Carolyn Swift

CAROLYN SWIFT worked as an actor, stage manager and director at the Gate and Pike theatres, before joining the Abbey Theatre board. She has also worked as a script writer and script editor at RTE, and has written plays, puppet plays, screen plays, as well as many children's books. Her books include the *Robbers* series and the *Bugsy* series. She also writes as dance critic for *The Irish Times*. Archaeology is one of her favourite hobbies. She has written two adventure books for children set in some of the world's most fascinating archaeological sites: *The Mystery of the Mountain*, set in Machu Picchu, and *The Secret City*, set in Petra, both available from The O'Brien Press.

The Mystery of the Mountain

Carolyn Swift

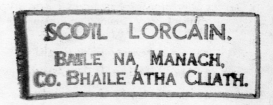

THE O'BRIEN PRESS
DUBLIN

This revised and re-edited edition published 1995 by
The O'Brien Press Ltd.,
20 Victoria Road, Rathgar, Dublin 6, Ireland
First published 1991

1 2 3 4 5 6 7 8 9 10
96 98 00 02 04 03 01 99 97 95

British Library Cataloguing-in-publication Data
Swift, Carolyn
Mystery of the Mountain
I. Title
823.914 [J]

ISBN 0-86278-413-1

The O'Brien Press receives assistance from
The Arts Council/An Chomhairle Ealaíon

Cover illustrations: Patrick Billington
Typesetting, editing, design, layout: The O'Brien Press Ltd.
Colour separations: Lithoset Ltd., Dublin
Printing: Cox & Wyman Ltd., Reading

CONTENTS

DEDICATION

This book is dedicated to the memory of my brother Harry Samuel, who was continually in my thoughts while I was writing it.

CHAPTER 1

The Strange Journey

Kevin had never been on such a strange train before. Firstly, it was so thin that there were only two rows of seats. Kevin's mother and his sister, Nuala, had to sit facing him on the other side of the narrow cramped carriage. Then, when the train had left San Pedro Station in Cuzco and climbed only a little way up the steep mountain, it gave a sort of jerk and stopped.

A fat woman with a shopping basket on her knee in the seat beside him didn't seem in the least bit worried by this, but Kevin was sure the train had broken down. Hardly surprising, he thought, considering how crowded it was. Some of the seats had three people squeezed into them and many more people were standing. Just when he had decided that the thin little train had definitely given up hope of hauling so many people up the mountain, the train gave a little shudder and started moving backwards. Alarmed, Kevin turned to look out the window behind him, thinking they must be rolling backwards down the hill into Cuzco. But no, they were still climbing.

As he watched the twin towers of San Pedro's church getting smaller and smaller behind them, the train shuddered to a halt yet again. He looked across to where Nuala and his mother were sitting and was just about to say something when the train jerked forward once more, throwing him back into his seat. Craning his neck to look down at the town, he saw Cuzco disappearing into the early morning mist below. The train was zig-zagging its way up the hill in the craziest manner, the same way the yachts tacked into Dun Laoghaire harbour when the wind was off the land. Now the city looked like an out-of-focus aerial photo. Through the morning mist Kevin could just pick out the dome and cupolas of the baroque Jesuit church of La Compañia. His mother had dragged them there the previous day to see its amazing altar and balconies, completely covered in gold.

The train started to move forward yet again, and the city disappeared behind them. They were rounding a bend in the mountain, which Kevin could see through a window on the far side of the carriage.

The mountain rose so steeply that you couldn't see its peak through the train window. Kevin kept expecting the train to stop again, but this time it kept going. Patches of yellow reminded him of the gorse-covered stretches of the Dublin mountains, though when he saw them close up, he realised the patches were not gorse but Scotch broom.

The mountain was quite different from any he had ever seen before. It was both higher and steeper than any mountain in Ireland and had spiky cactus plants and red and purple rocks showing here and there amongst the lush green vegetation. It was different from the Shera mountains around Petra in Jordan, where they had been last summer holidays, Kevin thought. Certainly those mountains had had plenty of cactus on them, but otherwise were bare and dry, so that you could walk anywhere you could find a foothold, so long as you watched out for prickles. These mountain slopes were so thickly covered that it would be almost impossible to cross them except where there were tracks. What would they find to do for three months in a place like this?

As the train reached the peak of the mountain, a thousand feet above the city, he could see roads stretching out in both directions below them and the remains of an old arched aquaduct which must once have carried water into Cuzco.

The train then crossed a great plateau. It looked disappointingly ordinary, with fields of wheat, barley and potatoes.

Kevin was beginning to think he might be sorry that he had agreed to spend the summer here. He and Nuala had had a really great time in Petra last year, once they'd made friends and found their way around, so he hadn't put up so much fight this year when his mother told him about her plans.

'You got on well enough with Amanda Houston in

the end, didn't you?' she had begun cautiously, remembering how strongly he had resisted going to Petra.

'She was okay,' Kevin admitted. 'Once she stopped doing the superior Yank bit. Why?'

'Because her father's heading up an international archaeological team on a dig in Peru this summer,' his mother told him. 'And he's offered me a place on it ...'

'... and I suppose if Nuala and I won't go with you for the holidays you'll lose the chance of a lifetime,' Kevin finished for her.

'Not necessarily,' said his mother sharply. 'Peru's a lot further away than Jordan and rather a dangerous place nowadays. There's a terrorist group, the *Sendero Luminosa* –'

'The what?' Kevin cut in.

'Maoist-type guerrillas,' his mother told him. 'They call themselves *Sendero Luminosa*. That's Spanish for "The Shining Path". So if you came with me you wouldn't be able to go wandering about on your own like you did in Petra. You'd have to stick pretty close to base. That's why I asked how you felt about Amanda, because you'd be thrown together a good deal.'

'Maybe I could go to Trabolgan with Joe and Jerry instead,' Kevin suggested hopefully.

'Ah, Kevin,' his mother sighed, 'you know that's not on. I can't possibly expect their mother to take responsibility for *you* as well. Besides, they're only going for a fortnight and I'd have to find somewhere that would take you for three months. I was thinking of sending you and Nuala to a summer school.'

'I'm not spending the whole holiday at school!' Kevin snapped.

'It wouldn't be like an ordinary school,' his mother explained patiently. 'There would be a lot of sport and maybe painting and music.'

'You don't care what we do as long as you get rid of us for the summer,' Kevin declared in disgust.

'You know that's not true,' his mother replied. 'I'm only worried about what you'd do with yourselves all day if you came with me.'

'We found plenty to do last year,' Kevin retorted, remembering how they had ridden out into the desert and gone snorkling in Aquaba.

'This will be very different,' his mother told him. 'We won't be surrounded by caves to explore, like in Petra, and we'll be miles from the sea. The dig's half-way up the side of a mountain!'

'Have you asked Nuala?' Kevin inquired.

He was willing to bet that she had. Women always stuck together. He should have had a father to side with him. It just wasn't fair that his father was dead.

'She wants to come,' his mother answered. 'But then she's not as keen on sports as you are.'

'It would do her good to play more games,' Kevin snarled. 'She's getting fat!'

'Kevin!' his mother snapped. 'Stop that. It's just a phase she's going through and you're not to be going on at her about it. She's self-conscious enough as it is.

Anyway, I told her I couldn't take her on her own. Either both of you come, or neither of you.'

'It's not fair!' Kevin shouted. 'I never have a real choice!'

When he started thinking about it, though, he began to really look forward to the trip.

Their journey had started with a long plane trip to Lima, the capital of Peru, where it had always seemed about to rain but never did. The pavements were so cracked and full of large holes that you were afraid to look up in case you tripped and broke a leg. Then, before they had properly got over their jet lag, they had had to board another plane for Cuzco.

There they had stayed for two nights, to get used to the altitude, his mother had said. Kevin only knew he had felt really odd. It was not just the sick feeling in his stomach, but also the fact that, every so often, the ground under his feet suddenly seemed to tilt and the walls of the room revolve.

'That's because we're so high up,' his mother had explained. 'Remember we're over eleven thousand feet above sea level. I feel a bit dizzy too. The guide book says we must take it very easy for a day or so.'

'I can't breathe properly,' Nuala complained. Her fair skin had gone as white as a sheet and she was panting as they climbed the stairs to their rooms.

'That's another symptom of altitude sickness,' her mother said. 'You should lie down on the bed for a while. And we must eat very little. Just a bowl of soup or something light like scrambled eggs.'

But the last thing Kevin wanted to do was to lie down. He had seen nothing of Lima and he would see nothing of Cuzco either if he did as his mother told him. He was not going to spend half the day in his room because of a little dizziness. Nuala could lie down if she liked, but he was going to slip out and explore. He waited until his mother left the room, then he put the bulky door key into the pocket of his jeans and set off back down the stairs.

He had almost reached the foot of the stairs when another wave of dizziness swept over him. He swayed, put out a hand for the bannisters and missed them. He would have fallen if a man had not caught him.

'Where you go?' the man asked.

Kevin tried hard to focus on him.

'Just out,' he muttered, as the walls steadied up a little and the stairs stopped tilting. 'I want to have a look around the place.'

'Not go like this,' the man said, shaking his head. 'You sick now. In one–two days you better. Maybe in one–two hours if you drink coca tea.'

'You mean I only have to drink tea!' Kevin exclaimed, thinking what a good laugh he would have at his mother if the sickness could be cured so easily.

'Special tea,' the man told him.

'Where do I get it?' Kevin asked eagerly.

'Come,' the man said, leading Kevin into a room off the hall. There was a bar counter at one end of the room, and two men were leaning against it drinking beer. At the other side of the room were small tables, and the man led Kevin over to one of these.

'You have money?' he asked.

Kevin was not so dizzy that he had forgotten all the warnings about pickpockets and con-men in strange cities. The man was dark-skinned with straight black hair and big brown eyes. He seemed nice and friendly, but it was as well to be careful.

'Not very much,' said Kevin, truthfully, for his mother had only given Nuala and himself a small amount of pocket money when she had cashed a traveller's cheque at the airport.

'Not need much,' the man laughed.

He called out to the barman in a language Kevin had never heard before. Of course he didn't understand Spanish, except for words like *gringo*, *amigo* and *mañana*, which he knew from telly westerns, but the sound of it was familiar to him from hearing it all around him ever since they had arrived in Peru. He was quite certain that this man wasn't speaking Spanish.

After a few minutes the barman came over with a cup and saucer, which he put down on the table. It was the weakest-looking tea Kevin had ever seen. There was no milk or sugar on the table, so he guessed he must be expected to drink it the way it was.

He took a small, cautious sip. It had a strange, but not unpleasant, flavour. He took another sip. The man was watching him, smiling.

'You drink all,' he told him. 'Then you pay barman. I go now.'

'Thank you,' Kevin said.

As the liquid cooled a little, he swallowed a large mouthful and then another. The effect was magical. The dizzy feeling left him completely and he walked steadily across to the bar with his fistful of small and crumpled notes. The barman took one from him.

'Now you are better, yes?' he asked.

Kevin grinned and nodded.

'If sickness come back you ask in café for coca tea,' the barman told him. 'Anywhere in Cuzco you get it.'

Delighted with himself, Kevin set off to explore the city. He passed stalls heaped with strange, brightly coloured fruit and vegetables, and a square where ice-cream vendors and shoe-shine boys were setting up their little stands. He glanced up steep, narrow alleyways leading off the street, some more like flights of steps than streets. There were clothes hanging out to dry on lines which ran between the two sides of some streets. There were people everywhere: a mixture of European and American tourists, and dark-skinned country people in loose woven jackets or ponchos. There were also Spanish-speaking men in well-cut light-weight suits, who Kevin decided must be Peruvian businessmen. Everyone was either buying or selling, staring up at the great walls of the town with their massive blocks of stone or fingering the woollen ponchos and rugs on the stalls. Kevin peered into shop windows full of burnished mirrors and candle-holders, wall-hangings and furry slippers, woven shoulder bags and belts.

After an hour or so he thought his mother might be starting to worry, so he found his way back to the hotel. He was just putting his key in the lock of his door when the door of the room opposite opened. His mother looked out.

'Where are you going?' she asked.

Kevin grinned. So she hadn't missed him at all!

'I'm not going anywhere,' he told her. 'I'm coming back. I was out giving the joint the once-over.'

'Kevin!' she cried. 'How many times have I told you not to go off on your own like that? Anything could have happened to you!'

'I didn't meet any guerrillas,' Kevin laughed. 'Only tourists and people selling things.'

'You might have taken a dizzy spell and fallen under a car,' she argued, but Kevin only laughed again.

'I'm not sick any more,' he told her. 'I had some coca tea and that fixed it.'

Now he had his mother's full attention. 'Nuala's still very sick and I had another dizzy spell just now,' she said. 'Maybe we could do with some of that.'

Kevin was sent to order coca tea for the three of them. When his mother and Nuala had each drunk a big cupful, they found that it worked as well for them as it had for Kevin. Only when a waiter came up to collect the tray did they ask what exactly it was.

'Made from leaf of coca plant,' he explained. 'Grows

high in mountains. All foreigners want try it. Sell for much money to Yankees.'

Kevin would never forget the look on his mother's face at that moment.

'Coca?' she cried in sudden realisation. 'D'you mean the leaves they make cocaine from? Have we been taking drugs?'

'All tourists drink coca tea,' the man muttered, making a hurried exit. 'Is only cure for mountain sickness.'

But Kevin's mother wouldn't be comforted.

'Promise me you'll never touch any of that dreadful stuff again!' she said to Kevin. 'Now you see what comes from going off on your own!'

In the dining-room over dinner, the tour guide with an English group told her that drinking coca-leaf tea really was a well-known cure for altitude sickness. It was very weak, he said, and not addictive if you drank it for a few days only. He did agree, however, that when made into cocaine it was a very dangerous drug indeed. Many people had died from taking it, he told Kevin and Nuala, even in England and Ireland.

Kevin was woken from his day-dreaming when the train stopped at a station. An old man wearing a funny pointy cap got into their carriage and squeezed himself in between Kevin and the woman with the shopping basket. Kevin, squashed up against the carriage partition, turned to complain and found that the old man was staring at him.

He had the same dark skin and straight black hair as

the man who had told him about the coca tea, but his face was deeply wrinkled and his almost black eyes were strangely piercing.

He muttered something which Kevin didn't understand, revealing a mouth in which at least half the teeth were missing. Unable to reply, Kevin just nodded and looked out the window again. The train was now entering a lovely sunlit valley, full of fruit trees. Here it stopped again and the woman with the basket got out. Kevin hoped the old man would move up and give him room to breathe, but instead more people squeezed into their carriage. A young man sat down where the woman had been. He said something to the old man who grinned back at him. Again Kevin couldn't place the language, but he felt sure it wasn't Spanish.

The train travelled along beside a river, in the middle of which he saw a great pillar, supporting the remains of a very old bridge. There were two huge rocks in front of the pillar, dividing the water so that it flowed on either side of it and not up against it. That must be why the pillar was still standing, Kevin figured, because the water was flowing very fast. The old man saw him staring at it.

'Inca bridge,' he said in English.

Kevin had heard his mother going on about the Incas. The dig they were going to was near an ancient city built by the Incas, he remembered. He tried to think what else she had told him about them. He thought she had said that they'd died out sometime in the sixteenth century, so they must have been great engineers to build something that was still standing in that fast-flowing river.

The old man tapped him on the arm. 'Inca terraces,' he said, pointing.

Kevin looked in the direction he was pointing and saw that the mountains beyond had been cut into great steps. Crops could be grown all the way up the steep slopes, on a series of wide terraces. The Incas must have been a bright lot, Kevin decided.

He smiled and nodded at the old man by way of thanks.

'Oh, Kevin, look!' Nuala called over to him. When he looked he saw one snow-capped mountain after another stretching into the distance as far as he could see.

'Deadly!' he called back. 'I'm going to climb the mountain at Machu Picchu!'

He heard the young man who had got on at the stop before last mutter something to the old man. They were speaking that same strange language.

'You go to Machu Picchu?' the old man asked Kevin. Kevin nodded.

'You not have time to climb mountain,' the old man told him. 'Tourist train leave again at three.'

'We're not tourists,' Kevin told him confidently. 'My mother has come here to work. She's an archaeologist and she'll be working on a dig there for three months. I'll have time to climb all the mountains around Machu Picchu.'

The man shook his head, almost angrily it seemed to Kevin. 'Huayna Picchu very dangerous,' he said.

'In my mother's guide book it says that there's a track all the way up,' Kevin argued. 'It says there are ruins at the top.'

'Track all washed away in rainy season,' the old man growled. 'Much tourists killed on that mountain.'

'The guide book didn't say that,' Kevin told him obstinately, as the train stopped again. A notice board on the platform advertised 'Hot Spring Baths', and a lot of people were getting out.

The young man was getting out too but, as he rose to his feet, he muttered something to the old man and shook his fist at Kevin. Kevin looked after him in surprise, wondering what he had done to annoy him, but the old man seemed angry too.

'I say mountain dangerous,' he growled again. 'You climb, you sorry! Ghosts of ancestors not welcome strangers. You stay away from mountain or bad thing happen!'

CHAPTER 2

The Distant Cry

When the train got to Puenta Ruinas Station the bus to take them up to Machu Picchu was waiting. Although the train was going on for another thirty-six miles to Chaullay, nearly everyone seemed to have got off with them. Many were obviously tourists. The station was full of people trying to sell them all sorts of things, from fruit to T-shirts with 'Machu Picchu' stencilled on them. One man kept following Nuala with a little musical instrument that was like a wooden version of a tin whistle. He would alternately play a few notes on it and then hold it out to her, and he kept following her until she gave him a really dirty look. Then he looked around until he saw another young girl, and tried to sell it to her.

Everyone jostled and shoved in the narrow space between the stalls which were packed tightly on every side. Nuala pushed her case into the luggage compartment of the bus and scrambled up the steps on the heels of her mother, to escape from all the traders. Her mother had managed to find two seats side-by-side, though the bus was already getting crowded. Then the man with the whistle came back. He kept tapping on the window beside them and holding up three fingers to show them the price. Nuala was glad when the doors of the bus swung shut, even though there were still people trying to cram on to it.

'Other bus comes,' the driver shouted, as the bus pulled away from the station with a splutter. They went across the bridge over the river and across the railway track. Then another crazy climb began, but this time, instead of the backwards and forwards zig-zags that the train had made, the bus laboured its way around hairpin bend after hairpin bend, swaying and lurching as it flung the passengers first to one side and then to the other.

'Gee!' cried a tall woman in the seat behind Nuala. 'Can you imagine what it must be like coming down? I bet he takes every one of these corners on two wheels. I reckon I'll just have to walk down!'

Nuala heard Kevin's laugh from across the bus. He was enjoying himself, she could see. It was clear that he wouldn't be walking down.

'There's a little track there that keeps crossing the road,' Nuala pointed out to her mother, as the bus rounded yet another bend. 'If you were walking you could come down that way. It would be a lot quicker.'

'It would, coming down,' her mother agreed, 'but I'm glad there's a bus for the way up. It's very steep. The guide book says it takes an hour on foot, though of course it's only a fraction of the distance it is by road because of the bends. It says here there are fourteen bends, and the road is five miles long.'

'That was as good as a go on the bumpers!' Kevin grinned, as they struggled out of the bus onto the flat space in front of the Hotel de Turistas.

Nuala looked all around her and gasped. They were on the edge of what looked like a gigantic serving dish, suspended in space as if it were a flying saucer. All around them the cliffs fell away steeply into a deep ravine, ringed by high mountains. The mountains seemed to be made out of heaps of Brussels sprouts, and Nuala couldn't tell if they were covered in small bushes or huge trees, because they were dwarfed by distance.

She turned to look behind her. The 'flying saucer' seemed to be moored to a mountain slope running up behind the hotel. She recognised the great mountain peak at once from the photo her mother had shown them back in Dublin. It was like a monster lying along the edge of the saucer, its head raised and its great mouth open, ready to gobble up anyone who was foolish enough to step too near. The smaller peak to the west of it formed the monster's lower jaw, and a great slab of rock between the two peaks looked like a protruding tongue.

'The mountain looks ready to swallow us all up!' Nuala gasped.

'What?' her mother asked, as she turned to see what Nuala was talking about. 'Oh, the mountain. There it is – Huayna Picchu. That means "Young Mountain" in Quechua, the language spoken by the Indians.'

'If that's a young mountain I wouldn't like to have to climb a middle-aged one!' Nuala giggled.

Then there was a shout from the direction of the hotel. 'Hi, Kevin! Nuala!'

Nuala turned to see Amanda Houston coming towards them and couldn't help feeling envy at the sight. Amanda was wearing khaki shorts which emphasised her long, slim legs, just as her crisp white cotton shirt stressed her cool blond elegance. In spite of the sun beating down on them, which made Nuala's face greasy, Amanda was wearing lipstick and looked perfectly groomed, as usual. She always looked much older than Kevin, thought Nuala, although at fifteen she actually came mid-way between herself and Kevin in age.

'Hi, Amanda,' she called, trying to sound enthusiastic.

Mr Houston appeared behind his daughter and hurried forward to greet them.

'Welcome aboard!' he cried to her mother, as if it really was a space ship they had just stepped on to, instead of the side of a mountain. 'Go right on in and relax for a while. I'll see to the baggage. Ask them what they wanna drink, Amanda, and put it on my tab.'

Nuala followed the others into the hotel lounge and sank gratefully into an armchair.

'Momma said to tell you hello!' Amanda drawled. 'And

she'll be right with you, soon as she takes her malaria tablets. Whadda you drinking?'

Nuala's mother looked around her doubtfully. The worn leather armchairs against the wall and the cheap tubular chairs at the tables gave the place a seedy, old-fashioned look.

'What have they got?' she asked.

'Pisco sour,' Amanda recommended without hesitation. 'It seems to be the local speciality. Momma drinks it all the time. And I guess Kevin and Nuala will have cokes, right?'

'I could murder a coke this minute,' Kevin agreed, slumping into one of the armchairs. Without giving anyone else time to agree or disagree, Amanda headed for the bar.

'I wish we had a house here, like we did in Petra,' Nuala said, looking over at a noisy group of people across the room. They were laughing and shouting and their table was heaped with beer bottles.

The idea of living in a hotel for three months seemed strange and this one looked unlikely to have even a games room, let alone a swimming pool.

'I know,' her mother agreed, 'but there's really nowhere but the hotel that could take us.'

'Here's Mrs Houston now,' Nuala said, as an older and slightly dried-up-looking version of Amanda appeared in the doorway.

'Well, hallo there!' she cried enthusiastically as she joined them. 'Am I glad to see a friendly face! Looks like we all drew the short straw this year. I was only telling Chuck this morning that I don't know how long I'm gonna be able to take this joint. I was thinking of maybe flying on to Rio with Amanda for a week or two, but I guess you'll be spending too much time at Machu Marca to care if it's all a bit grotty.'

'What's Machu Marca?' Kevin asked.

'It means "Old City" in Indian language,' Mrs Houston told him. 'It's the name Chuck's given to the ruins of a city he reckons is on the far side of the mountain. That's what your mother will be helping to excavate.'

Amanda rejoined them, sitting languidly on the arm of Kevin's chair. 'The drinks are coming right up,' she said.

'Ask them to add a pisco sour for me too, will you, honey?' her mother ordered, but Amanda only laughed.

'That's coming right up too,' she said. 'And I ordered Poppa a beer.'

'You gotta be psychic,' Mr Houston grinned, dropping hotel keys down on the table, 'but I hope you didn't just say "*cerveza*"!'

'No, Poppa. I asked for your special. Look, here it comes.'

Nuala inspected the tray that the waiter set down on the table – three cokes, two smaller glasses containing a pale liquid with froth on top, and one unusual-looking beer bottle.

'*Chicha de Jora*,' she read out loud. 'Is that Peruvian beer?'

'Better than that,' Mr Houston told her. 'It's Inca beer, made from fermented corn.'

'Sounds more like spirits,' Kevin commented.

Mr Houston shook his head. 'It's not distilled. It kinda takes a bit of getting used to, but I guess we have to get into the spirit of the Incas in every way we can.'

Kevin and Nuala's mother took a cautious sip of her pisco sour and then exclaimed: 'This stuff's wonderful! What do they put in it?'

'It's a local grape brandy,' Mrs Houston told her, 'with ice, lemon, bitters and a little egg. Strong stuff, and one's probably more than enough at this hour, but I reckon we could all do with a little pick-me-up right now.'

'Can I have a taste?' Kevin pleaded, but his mother moved her glass firmly out of his reach.

'You had quite enough strange drinks in Cuzco,' she told him. 'I suppose I'd better go and see to the cases.'

'It's all taken care of,' Mr Houston told her. 'They're taking them up to the rooms, but really, there's no need to hurry. The Spanish and the Conquistadors may have been here, but I don't think Speedy Gonzales ever made it! They really believe in taking their time up here. Look, why don't I show you around Machu Picchu before lunch and then you can lie down for an hour or so. You wanna take things easy today, because the jeep leaves at seven sharp tomorrow morning.'

As soon as they had finished their drinks, they all set out along a track leading from the hotel to the ancient city of Machu Picchu. It was only a short walk to the entrance gate to the city at the top of the steps. Nuala was surprised to see a group of thatched cottages and barns just inside the gate.

'They're like old farm buildings at home!' she exclaimed.

'They've been restored,' Mr Houston explained, 'so people can see what they would have looked like when they were built in the early fifteenth century. But look at the walls!'

'What about them?' Kevin asked.

'You can always identify an Inca building by its walls,' Mr Houston told him. 'See how they fitted the irregular stones so cleverly that they've held together all these years without mortar!'

'But *are* they farm buildings?' Nuala persisted.

'I guess they are,' Mr Houston answered. 'The houses were the homes of the Caretakers of the Terraces, but since the terraces were for agriculture I reckon you could call the caretakers farmworkers. And the other buildings would have been for storing grain.'

Nuala thought that if this was all there was to see in Machu Picchu it was no match for the rock-cut palace tombs of Petra. But, when they followed the path through the houses and out on to a raised track running along the top of the city wall, she gasped at the view in front of her. Now they were on the open mountainside once more and the ground fell away steeply below the wall in a series of wide steps that covered the whole section of mountain.

'These are the terraces,' Mr Houston told them. 'Once upon a time they would have been full of potatoes.'

'Just like at home,' Kevin said.

'Ah, but the Incas grew potatoes five hundred years before they were brought to Europe,' he answered. 'And they also grew over two hundred other kinds of vegetables, fruits and herbs.'

'And all without ploughing,' Kevin commented. 'They'd never get a tractor up here!'

Mr Houston didn't let it go at that. 'They ploughed all the same,' he said.

'I can't see how,' Kevin argued. 'Not even a horse-drawn plough would be any good up here. The terraces are only three or four feet wide, and how would they get up and down the steps?'

'The Incas had no horses,' Mr Houston told him. 'They'd never even seen one until the Spanish arrived and at first they thought that horse and rider were one being. They ploughed by hand, using a *chaqui-taclla*.'

'A what?' Kevin asked.

'A wooden stick tipped with metal and operated by a foot stirrup,' Mr Houston explained.

Nuala stood looking away into the distance. Even here she felt as if she were somehow hovering above the valley. It was approaching mid-day by now, and the sun was beating straight down on the terraces. Nuala's T-shirt clung to her and the sweat ran down her face. She was fishing in the pocket of her jeans for a tissue when she realised the others had gone on. They were disappearing through a gap in the wall which marked the end of the terraces.

She hurried after them but gave up half-way across. It was just too hot for running. At a slow walk now, she had almost reached the wall leading straight down the mountainside when a strange white head suddenly loomed up over the top of it right in front of her. Nuala let out a little squeal as it went on rising like a sea serpent coming up out of the waves. Then she heard a laugh and a man appeared through the gap in the wall.

'*Das ist nur ein alpaca,*' he said. '*Kommen Sie!*'

Nuala didn't understand what he said, as she didn't speak German, but she was delighted to see a fellow human being and followed his beckoning hand through the gap. Then she too burst out laughing. On the far side of the wall were three white woolly animals. They were sort of like sheep, but with long necks which seemed to extend like a periscope when they wanted to see over the top of something, as their leader was doing now. Suddenly Nuala remembered seeing something like them in the Dublin Zoo, gazing at her through the bars of an enclosure. She remembered the same pricked ears and startled expression that had alarmed her just now.

'Oh, llamas!' she laughed.

The man shook his head. '*Nein,*' he said. '*Nicht llama. Alpaca.*'

'I thought that was the stuff they made men's suits out of,' Nuala answered, but the man obviously didn't understand English. After looking at her blankly for a moment, he tipped his Panama hat politely and moved away up a long flight of steps.

Nuala realised she had left the farming district and entered the city of Machu Picchu itself. All about her now were the remains of houses. The odd one had a thatched roof, but mostly they were no higher than her shoulder and she could see that they hadn't been rebuilt. Since she could see over most of the walls, she thought it should be easy to see Kevin and the others. She looked all around but, though there were groups of tourists everywhere, clustered about their guides, there was no sign of Kevin or her mother. The tourists in the distance looked like midgets against the gigantic peak of Huayna Picchu. Then she heard her name being called from above. She saw her mother coming out of a thatched house a little further on, half-way up another flight of steps.

'Hurry-up, slow coach!' her mother called, as Nuala hurried on and up the steep steps to join her. 'You're missing the fountains.'

'Where?' Nuala asked eagerly, looking forward to the splash of cool water.

'All the way down beside the steps here,' her mother told her, pointing.

'You mean those little walled boxes?' Nuala asked, disappointed.

'The water ran down from one into the other,' her mother explained. 'There are sixteen of them and each held a fountain. The water rises half a mile away in the mountains.'

'But where *is* the water?' Nuala asked. 'Does it dry up in the summer or something?'

'It all goes to the hotel now,' her mother said. 'Otherwise there'd be none in the taps. Come on, or we'll be left behind.'

'You go on,' Nuala told her. 'I can't hurry in this heat, and everything seems to be up steps.'

'Yes, there's a lot of steps all right,' her mother agreed. 'Mr Houston said there are more than three thousand of them, divided into a hundred flights of stairs.'

'Then I think I'll leave them for another day,' Nuala said. 'I've ages to see it all while you're working.'

'Go on back then,' her mother nodded. 'We'll be going back for lunch ourselves in an hour or so. I'll see you in the hotel,' she said, hurrying off up the steps to catch up with the others.

Going down the steps was less tiring than going up and Nuala began to feel a little better. There was no need to hurry now. When she reached the track they had come along, Nuala saw that it continued on across the landing of yet another flight of steps and out towards a green grassy area. She decided to head for there.

When she finally reached the spot she had picked out, which was rather further than it had looked, it turned out to be a huge lawn. She wondered how they got mowing machines over to it and then realised it had been mown by the chomping jaws of those strange woolly creatures, the alpaca. It was quiet and peaceful, though she could still hear tourists above, below and behind her. Their voices sounded fainter from here as they hurried up and down stairways and in and out of the remains of houses. The sandy track she had just come down was deserted.

Leaning against a wall of great rectangular stones, worn smooth over the centuries, Nuala thought the mountain looked even more mysterious now that she was closer to it. She could even see, high up, almost at the top, terraces like the one she had crossed earlier. There had to be a track up to them, even though the cliff face looked almost sheer and covered in thick undergrowth. Maybe when you got closer you could see the track. She would go just a little further before turning back.

The sandy track she was following began to curve off to the right and downwards above a sheer drop. It was fenced off by a rough wooden rail. It struck Nuala that the further down she went the further she would have to climb back up again when she turned back. She had gone far enough. She stopped and with one hand on the rail for support, took a last look up at the mountain.

Now even the distant sounds of tourists' voices were stilled. The great peak seemed to float against the sky in majestic silence, a wisp of soft thin cloud momentarily hiding its face. Then suddenly, from far away, came a high-pitched, despairing cry. It echoed off the mountain and then ended, as abruptly as if it had been switched off.

Nuala's hand tightened on the wooden rail. Even in

the heat of the mid-day sun, there was something about that cry that gave her a cold feeling in the pit of her stomach. It was probably only a bird, she told herself. There were lots of strange birds in the Andes, whose calls she didn't know. All the same, hot and tired though she was, she began to run back the way she had come, towards the safety of the hotel.

CHAPTER 3

The Lonely Climb

By the time they had unpacked that evening Nuala was exhausted.

'It's the altitude,' her mother said, 'and all the travelling is tiring too. Lie down on the bed and have a rest.'

Even Kevin didn't have the strength to argue and after they had all rested there was only time for what their mother called 'a short walk' before the light faded. Nuala didn't consider it a short walk at all. They went to look at the view from the old Inca road linking Machu Picchu with the next Inca city. Even that meant going as far as the end of the terraces, where she had seen the alpaca, and then climbing almost to the top of the first flight of steps.

They passed through a great stone gateway, which her mother said had been the main entrance to the city in Inca times. Then they were faced with yet more steps. By the time they reached the top of these, and stood finally on the mountain track her mother said was the

Inca road, Nuala was as hot and tired as she had been at lunchtime.

'Do we have to go much further?' she asked, mopping her face with a tissue.

'The walk to Huinay Huayna takes two-and-a-half hours,' her mother laughed, 'so I don't think we'll do that now.'

'To *where?*' Kevin asked.

'It means "For Ever Young". It must be the Indian version of "*Tír na nÓg*",' his mother said.

'Does that mean it's not really there?' Nuala asked.

'Oh no, it's there all right,' her mother told her. 'Apparently it has terraces of houses like the ones here, and a great circular wall of huge stones, all built on top of a precipice beside a gigantic waterfall. It sounds wonderful and I'd love to go there one day, but it would be a full day's expedition, because you can only get there on foot. In any case, we haven't seen a quarter of Machu Picchu yet.'

'Oh, I'm in no hurry,' Kevin assured her, looking along the mountain track, which led diagonally upwards and disappeared over the shoulder of the mountain.

'Wow! We're high up!' Nuala gasped, turning to look down at the valley.

'Not as high as we were in Cuzco,' her mother pointed out. 'It's just that the climb from the hotel is so steep and the hotel itself is two thousand feet above the station. Imagine what it must have been like getting up here before they built the road in 1948! But then the Incas

36

didn't often come from down there. They came this way, from Huinay Huayna.'

'It's almost a sheer drop to the valley,' Kevin said. 'D'you think if I fell I'd roll all the way down?'

'I wouldn't try to find out,' his mother remarked dryly.

'Look at the mountain opposite,' Nuala cried, 'on the other side of the valley. It's so green!'

'I expect that's the tea plantation,' her mother told her. 'Apparently they're famous for the quality of their tea. That at least should be good here, even if the hotel food isn't very exciting.'

So it was over their tea that Kevin and Nuala were lingering the next morning. Their mother and Mr Houston had gone to the dig and the tourists had all hurried off to cram in as much time as they could in Machu Picchu before leaving for the three o'clock train. Tourists never seemed to stay more than one night. In fact, most of them came over from Cuzco just for the day.

'And is it any wonder,' Kevin remarked, 'considering the food and the way all the lights cut out an hour or so after dinner, so you can't even read?'

'I should think they're all too tired to even want to,' Nuala replied, as she watched a waiter, busy loading the dirty delph from the table next to them on to a tray.

Suddenly the hotel manager hurried out from the kitchen. He seemed very excited and ran over to the waiter, speaking to him urgently in a voice too low for Nuala to overhear. She saw the waiter's expression change to one of shock. Though his skin was dark, he seemed nevertheless to turn pale and his hands shook so much that the cups on his tray began to rattle. The manager took the tray from him and put it down on the table. Placing an arm around his shoulders, he led him from the room, leaving the tray behind.

'Did you see that?' Nuala asked Kevin. 'Something awful must have happened.'

'Looks like it,' Kevin agreed.

Then the manager returned for the tray. Before he could leave again with it, Kevin spoke. 'Is something wrong?'

The manager looked at him uneasily. 'I tell José his brother dead,' he said finally. 'His cousin find body on way to plantation this morning.'

'That's awful!' Nuala cried. 'Did he have a heart attack or something?'

A sudden rage swept over the man. 'They kill him!' he shouted. 'They throw him off mountain and kill him!'

'Who killed him?' Kevin asked. 'Was it the *Sendero Luminosa*?'

The manager gave him a frightened glance, shook his head and, without replying, hurried from the room.

'If he doesn't know who it was, how can he be so sure it was murder?' Kevin muttered. 'He might just have slipped and fallen.'

'Maybe there was a bullet hole in his body,' Nuala answered, 'or a knife wound. Anyway, I think he does know but he's afraid to say. He didn't want to talk about it at all, only he got too angry to keep his mouth shut.

He looked really scared when you asked him about the guerrillas.'

'Then it probably *was* them,' Kevin said. 'D'you think they're over on the mountain across the valley, where the tea plantation is?'

Suddenly Nuala remembered the cry she had heard the day before. For a second she felt sick.

'What's wrong?' Kevin asked, as she clapped her hand over her mouth, her stomach heaving.

'I don't think it happened across the valley,' she whispered. 'I think it was on Huayna Picchu.'

'But he said the cousin was on his way to the plantation when he found the body,' Kevin said. 'There's no tea growing on Huayna Picchu, is there?'

'I don't know,' Nuala said, 'but I think it was there all the same.'

'Why?' Kevin asked.

'Because I think I know when it happened,' Nuala whispered. 'I think I heard him scream as he fell.'

After she had told him exactly where she had been and what she had heard, Kevin sat for a moment in stunned silence. When he finally spoke he was unusually serious.

'I hope you're wrong,' he said, 'because Mum's working on Huayna Picchu.'

Nuala looked at him in horror. Why had she not thought of that? There was only one thing to do.

'We must warn her,' she said.

Amanda stuck her head into the dining-room. 'Are

you guys still here?' she teased. 'If you don't shift soon they'll be serving lunch!'

'We're going now,' Kevin answered, 'so you can tell your mother we won't be here for lunch. It's probably scraggy old chicken again anyway.'

'But you're too late for a packed lunch now,' Amanda told them. 'You gotta order it the night before. Where are you heading?'

'To the dig,' Nuala said, 'and we couldn't order last night because we've only just decided to go.'

'But you don't even know the route,' Amanda protested.

'Can't we ask one of the guides to tell us the way?' Kevin retorted.

'I wouldn't trust them with a nickel,' Amanda said. 'They're a pack of twisters. Wait till after lunch and *I'll* guide you. Poppa took me half-way there the day before yesterday. And he gave me a map with the Temple of the Moon marked on it.'

'Thanks,' Nuala said, 'but we have to go now.'

'Only we *could* use a map,' Kevin added. 'Will you give us a loan of it?'

'I'd rather come with you,' Amanda replied. 'I'm blue mouldy from hanging around with Momma. She does nothing but bellyache because there's no horseback riding. But I sure ain't setting out on a long trek on an empty stomach. Hang on while I get us a packed lunch.'

'But you said it was too late,' Nuala pointed out.

'Yeah,' Amanda said, 'but I bet I can sweet-talk José

into doing it for me. He likes me, I guess.'

Before anyone could argue with her, Amanda had marched off through the swing-door into the kitchens.

'I don't think she ought to come,' Nuala said. 'I mean, it might be dangerous and ... well, you know.'

'If Amanda's made up her mind you won't stop her,' Kevin argued. 'Anyway, we need the map and the lunch and it looks like we won't get either without her.'

'I suppose she has a right to come,' Nuala agreed, 'when her dad's there too. But she's always talking – we'd better warn her to keep her mouth shut.'

'Say nothing for the moment,' Kevin suggested. 'She can't give away what she doesn't know. Besides, if Mrs Houston hears about all of this she'll stop us going.'

So it was that Amanda still knew nothing about their mission as, half an hour later, with their lunch in a rucksack on Amanda's back the three of them set off through the old city.

When they reached Nuala's lawn, Amanda told her it was called the 'Esplanade'. The herd of alpaca were grazing there and Nuala told Amanda how they had scared her the day before.

'And I thought they were llamas,' she concluded. 'They look a bit like the llamas in Dublin Zoo.'

'Alpaca are fatter and woollier than llamas,' said Amanda, 'though they're the same family. Poppa says they're worth more, on account of you can make ordinary sweaters and ponchos out of llama wool but you gotta have alpaca for real expensive suiting. You don't see the peasants driving alpaca with goods on their backs to market, like they do the llamas.'

'I haven't seen anybody driving llamas,' Nuala protested. 'In fact, I haven't seen any ordinary people since we got here, only hotel staff, guides and tourists.'

'I reckon you will when we get near the dig,' Amanda told her. 'There's gotta be folks working on the lower slopes on the far side of the mountain.'

Nuala followed Amanda along the sandy track she had taken the day before. Even though it was much earlier in the day she could feel the heat in the sun.

'It's getting hot already,' she said.

'Wait till we get climbing,' Amanda laughed. '*That'll* be hot work, I'm telling you.'

When they reached the point where the track began to run downhill around the edge of the precipice, Nuala stopped. 'This is where I heard the scream,' she said.

Kevin stopped and looked over the rail at the steep drop below them and then up at the towering peak ahead.

'It's hard to believe there's a track up there,' he said finally.

'There's steps,' Amanda told them, 'but you can't see them on account of they're covered in vegetation. What's all that about a scream, Nuala?'

Kevin shook his head in warning and Nuala hesitated. 'I thought it might be someone in trouble,' she said, 'but it must have been a bird.'

'What d'ya bet it was a condor,' Amanda said. 'They've

a harsh cry that's real scary. They're as big as eagles and Poppa says they're real scavengers. If a new-born llama is sickly they'll try picking him off from the herd. They'll stick around for days, aiming to drive the mother off. Then they'll pick his bones clean as a whistle!'

Nuala shuddered. The mountains were beginning to sound like cruel and frightening places.

'That's horrid,' she said.

'They're kinda like vultures, I guess,' Amanda shrugged. 'Poppa says it keeps the mountains clean of rotting flesh when anything dies. But he said never to go climbing these mountains alone on account of if you slipped and broke a leg the condors would get you.'

Nuala shuddered again, hoping José's brother was dead before the condors reached him. Her throat felt dry as she thought about it. Then she remembered her mother.

'Come on,' she shouted. 'Let's go!'

'Sure,' Amanda drawled, 'you're the one that keeps stopping.'

They skirted the great slab of rock that Nuala had imagined as the projecting tongue of a monster. Now they were about to enter his gaping jaws!

'There's the track,' Amanda told her.

Nuala looked at it in horror as they started to climb. It went up the inside of the upper jaw of the monster's mouth in a series of zig-zags, curves and bends, so you could only see tiny sections of it here and there. It began as a rough path. Then it became steps, crumbling where they cut across dry rock and the heat of the sun had dried them, slippery with wet and rotting leaves where they were overshadowed by creeper.

'Why's it so wet?' Nuala called out, concentrating on keeping her footing.

'We're right on the edge of the jungle,' Amanda called back. 'Poppa says Machu Picchu was all jungle until the Incas cleared it for building, and after they abandoned it the jungle grew right up over it again. Hiram Bingham, who discovered it in 1911, must have had to cut away the creeper before he could be sure it was there.'

Clinging tightly to an overhanging branch, Nuala turned to look back at the ruins below them. Apart from the light green of the Esplanade, everything, even the stone walls, seemed tinged with the same lush green that she could see on the mountains opposite.

'What's that funny thing over there on the top?' Nuala asked. 'That thing sticking up like a sundial?'

Kevin's voice echoed down to her from somewhere out of sight. He was on the far side of a rock above and to the left of her.

'We were up there yesterday after you split,' he said. 'Amanda's Dad thinks it probably *is* a sort of a sundial. It's called Inti-something-or-other.'

'*Intihuatana*.'

It was Amanda's voice this time and Nuala noticed with disgust that she didn't even sound out of breath. It was maddening that she not only looked like a model but was athletic as well.

'It means "the place where the sun is tied" in the Indian language,' Amanda continued. 'Inti was the name of the sun god. Poppa says the Inca High Priest told the people at the winter solstice that the sun couldn't go away any further because he had tied it to that stone. He was real smart. He knew that at the solstice the sun would return from the north, but the people thought it was his magic that did it. The Spaniards were pretty smart too. When they realised the Incas worshipped the sun and that the Intihuatana had something to do with it, they destroyed them all.'

'So how come that one's still there?' It was Kevin's voice again.

'Because the Spaniards never found Machu Picchu,' Amanda called back. 'Only the Indians knew it was here until Hiram Bingham got here. That's why he called it "The Lost City of the Incas".'

'So it's a secret city too, like Petra,' Nuala cried, as she struggled on reluctantly after the others.

If she hadn't been so worried about her mother, Nuala would probably have given up after half-an-hour. Sometimes she could only get to the next step by clinging to the undergrowth and praying that it would hold as she stretched across the gap. She had no idea how much further it was to the top and she knew by the sound of their voices that the distance between herself and the others was lengthening.

She could neither see the others nor the top of the mountain above her, because of the way the steps were cut into the angles of the rock. The only time she tried to look up, dry soil rained down on her face, dislodged by Amanda's shoes on the bend above. Only by taking an occasional fearful glance behind her could she tell how high she was from the top of the smaller peak to the west, now well below her. She no longer dared to look at Machu Picchu itself. Suddenly Kevin's voice reached her from what seemed like a long way above.

'I'm on the terrace!' he cried triumphantly.

Encouraged, Nuala struggled on. It would be easier going once they were out on the open mountainside again and she knew from seeing them from the ground that the terraces were near the mountaintop. Gasping for breath, her eyes smarting from the sweat that ran down into them, she clambered across a space where the steps had worn away again. Then she scrambled up a few more steps, pulled herself by the branches of a small shrub around a bend and suddenly found herself on the flat green space beneath the first terrace wall.

'Thank God!' she gasped. 'I thought I'd never make it!'

With one last effort, she managed to hoist herself up on to the top of the wall and, almost sobbing with relief, rolled over until she was sitting on the step, her legs dangling over the large, smooth stones.

In front of her there was only space. In the far distance was the dark outline of a mountain range, but it was so far away it looked indistinct and hazy. When she looked down she could see a series of lines and squares and a few circles far below, like a strange wallpaper pattern, which she knew marked the ruined city of Machu Picchu. A greyish lump to the west of it could only be the smaller peak she had thought of as the lower jaw of the monster, now flattened by her bird's eye view of it. Beside it, a smaller grey lump had to be the great tilted slab of rock she had thought of as the monster's tongue. Now she must be sitting just below his upper lip!

No sounds reached her from below, even though by now there must be thousands of sightseers in the ruins. The feeling of isolation was terrifying. She was glad she was not alone.

For the first time she turned to look upward, expecting to see Kevin and Amanda somewhere above her on the terraces. To her horror, she saw nothing but a series of great steps faced by stone walls, rising above her towards the peak, which seemed to swim against the sky, making her feel dizzy. In sudden panic she realised that there was not another being in sight.

CHAPTER 4

The Skeleton in the Cave

'Kevin!' Nuala screamed in sudden panic. 'Kevin!' The sound of her voice echoed back to her from the rocky wall above in a hollow, mocking way. She looked in every direction, her terror growing. She had heard Kevin's voice ahead of her just a moment before. If anything had happened to him surely she would have heard him cry out? Yet he was nowhere to be seen and it looked like Amanda had vanished as well. They had disappeared from sight on and off all the way up but here, on the open terrace, it seemed impossible that she couldn't see them.

It was as if they had dissolved into the thin mountain air, which was beginning to make her heart pound the way it had when they had first arrived in Cuzco. Nuala looked down once more at the ruins, a thousand feet or so below, her head swimming. The thought of being alone on this monster mountain was almost as frightening as the fear that something might have happened to Kevin.

'Hi, Nuala!' Nuala jumped. Kevin's voice came from somewhere behind her. Her eyes burned with tears of relief. She turned and saw him standing at the far end of the terrace.

'Kevin,' she cried, 'where were you? I looked *everywhere*. And where's Amanda?'

'Come and see,' he shouted back.

Nuala's legs ached, her shirt was soaked with sweat and her breath still seemed to tear at her throat, but she needed to be with the others. The feeling of being suspended in space, a solitary and insignificant object no bigger than a fly, had been terrible. She couldn't wait to stand beside Kevin and Amanda and feel normal-sized again. Summoning up all her energy, she struggled across the terraces to join them.

'Now,' Kevin ordered, 'close your eyes!'

'Don't act the maggot!' she begged. 'I'm too tired. If you disappear on me again I'll scream!'

'I won't!' he promised. 'Just shut your eyes for a sec.'

As she closed them, Kevin pulled her around to face the mountain.

'Now you can open them,' he said.

Nuala found herself looking into a hole in the side of the mountain. It might once have been a natural cleft in the rocks, but it had been hollowed out into a sort of tunnel. Creepers hung over the mouth of the tunnel, making it impossible to see unless you were up close to it. Just inside, sitting on her rucksack, was Amanda.

Nuala looked at her in disbelief. She was sitting in the

shade, as relaxed as if she were in a deck-chair, studying her map and drinking coke through a straw. Her shorts, Nuala noticed, were not even creased. It just wasn't fair!

'However did you find this place?' she gasped.

'Amanda's father showed it to her,' Kevin said. 'It was made by the Incas.'

Nuala entered the tunnel, eager to escape from the sun. She had begun to feel that she was melting like butter in a pan.

'Can I have my coke?' she begged Amanda. 'My tongue's all dried up.'

'Sure.' Amanda uncrossed her long legs, then slid off her rucksack and opened it up. She extracted another can of coke and a straw.

'I guess it got kinda warm with the sun on my back,' she apologised, 'but it's wet. D'you want your sandwich now?'

'I wouldn't mind,' Nuala said.

'Let's all eat now,' Kevin agreed. 'What did he give you?'

'Three guesses!'

Kevin groaned. 'Scraggy chicken?'

'You got it!' Amanda laughed, pulling out a greaseproof paper packet and throwing it across to him. 'But Momma always says hunger's a good sauce! And he gave us a mango each. They oughta be good and juicy. You can thank me that you got anything at all!'

Amanda was right about the hunger sauce, for Kevin ate his sandwiches without a word. When there was neither a crumb of food nor a drop of coke left, he got to his feet. 'I'll take the rucksack for a bit now if you like,' he offered.

'Now he says it!' Amanda laughed, stuffing the wrapping paper back into the rucksack. 'Now that it's empty and light! Thanks for nothing!'

'You wouldn't think it was funny if he was your brother,' Nuala told her. 'That's the sort of thing he *always* does.'

'Okay,' Kevin retorted. 'Carry it yourself, so, only don't say I didn't offer!'

He went back towards the mouth of the tunnel, but Amanda called after him: 'If you wanna go that way, fine. We'll meet up with you on the other side!'

Nuala stared at her in amazement.

'Are you saying this tunnel goes right through the mountain?' she asked.

'I *think* so,' Amanda replied. 'Poppa says it's well known that one of these tunnels goes through.'

Nuala peered doubtfully into the blackness ahead. 'If it went right through we'd see light from the other end,' she pointed out.

'Not if there's a bend in it,' Amanda told her.

'Why would there be a bend in it?' Nuala argued. 'They'd surely go the shortest way.'

'Not if there was hard rock in between,' Kevin put in. 'They'd cut through wherever it was softest. But if there are other tunnels, how do we know this is the one that goes through?'

'Poppa said the ones higher up didn't look like they went through,' Amanda replied, 'but by the time he'd examined the ruin at the top there was no time to explore the tunnels.'

'D'you mean the Incas built houses up above those terraces too?' Nuala cried. 'They must have been mad! Imagine climbing all the way up here to your house! But then they must have been mad to plant crops up here too.'

'Poppa reckons these were sacred gardens,' Amanda told her. 'He figures the tunnel was to link the Sacred Gardens and their temple with the Temple of the Moon.'

'Where's that?' Kevin asked.

'Near where the dig is,' Nuala said. 'Isn't that right, Amanda? On the other side of the mountain.'

'Yeah,' Amanda agreed, 'though it's not like the Temple of the Sun in the middle of Machu Picchu. It's really just a big cave, with niches cut in it.'

'Like the tombs at Petra!' Nuala cried in delight.

'Sorta like them, I guess,' Amanda agreed, 'except it's not like a palace on the outside.'

'If I was going to cut a tunnel through the mountain I'd cut it higher up, at the top of the terraces,' Kevin said, 'because it would be shorter higher up. I wonder why your dad is so sure this is the one that goes through?'

'He reckons they tried going through higher up and they either met hard rock or became scared the rock above would cave in,' Amanda told him. 'He figures that's what the ones higher up are – tunnels they started and abandoned, and they had to come down this far to get right through.'

'All the same,' Nuala said uneasily, 'we could waste an awful lot of time if we had to come back again.'

'It's up to you,' Amanda shrugged, 'but I'm going this way. And I thought you didn't want to do any more climbing?'

'Won't we have to climb on the other side anyhow?' Nuala argued.

Amanda shook her head. 'We go *down* on the other side,' she said. 'The Temple of the Moon's only halfway up and the dig's just below it on a small plateau.'

'You mean I've climbed all the way up here only to go most of the way down again?' Kevin cried in disgust.

'You gotta,' Amanda told him, 'unless you go in the jeep. But the way the jeep goes takes hours. You'd never do it on foot.'

'Then we may as well give the tunnel a try,' Kevin agreed.

'But it's pitch black and we haven't got a torch,' Nuala protested.

'I reckon our eyes will adjust once we get going,' Amanda said. 'I'll lead the way. Momma always says I've eyes like a cat.'

Nuala hesitated. It would certainly be less tiring if they went through the tunnel, provided it really did go through. She didn't fancy struggling up the final stretch of mountain in the full heat of the sun, but the thought of burrowing into the depths of the mountain filled her with a strange dread.

'Nuala's afraid she'll get stuck in the tunnel!' Kevin jeered.

Nuala flushed. 'I'm not *that* fat!' she snapped. 'You go ahead and I'll follow.'

So the little procession set off in single file, Amanda first, then Kevin, and Nuala last. As they groped their way forward along the tunnel, Nuala felt the ground rising under her feet and guessed they were going uphill, though she could see nothing. Even if it hadn't been dark in the tunnel there was nothing to see but Kevin's back, which now completely filled the space ahead of her. Amanda's voice, muffled and echoing, reached her.

'The roof's getting lower and lower,' she warned.

Nuala felt a growing sense of panic. They were completely trapped in that small dark tunnel. Her T-shirt felt cold and clammy against her ribs and she realised she was sweating worse than ever. The strange atmosphere was stifling, despite a dank chill. But turning back would be almost impossible now, for they were forced to crouch until they were like rabbits in a burrow.

There was nothing for it but to fight her fears and shuffle slowly on at Kevin's heels.

Then she heard Amanda's voice again. 'I've got to the bend,' it cried, recognisable though distorted. 'The passage is starting to slope down again too and ... hey! there's a speck of light ahead!'

'Deadly!' Kevin shouted. 'If I don't straighten up soon I'm going to be stuck this way for good!'

'We're gonna make it!' Amanda called back. 'The roof's rising too.'

Nuala felt, rather than saw, Kevin swinging to the left ahead of her and then she felt the ground falling away beneath her feet. She wished she could see the light but with two bodies in the way it was impossible. Still, she could stand upright once more. Soon this horrible game of follow-my-leader would be over and they would be out in the air again.

'Is it much farther?' she asked.

'I guess not,' Amanda called back. 'The light's getting stronger.'

Then Nuala heard her gasp. Before she could ask what was wrong, she had bumped into Kevin.

'You might have warned me you were going to stop like that!' she complained, holding her bumped nose.

'D'you think I wanted you to walk on my heel?' Kevin snapped. 'You can blame Amanda. She stopped without warning me.'

'Shh!' Amanda hissed.

'What's happening?' Nuala whispered.

'I think there's someone – or something – there!'

Nuala felt the back of her neck tingle. 'What d'you mean, some*thing*?' she croaked.

'Shh!' Amanda repeated urgently.

They crouched in silence, holding their breath for what seemed like ages.

'What can you see?' Nuala whispered after a while.

'Nothing now,' Amanda whispered back, 'but the light

was coming and going, as if something kept passing in front of it.'

'Oh no!' Nuala gasped. 'What could it be?'

'Maybe a deer,' Amanda told her. 'Poppa says there are deer and other wild animals on the far side of Machu Picchu.'

'Other wild animals?' Nuala echoed in horror. 'What sort of wild animals?'

'Bears and pumas and snakes and things like that,' Amanda replied.

'Snakes!' Nuala's voice rose to a shrill scream. 'Why didn't you say so before? The tunnel could be crawling with them! Are they poisonous?'

'I reckon so,' Amanda said. 'Let's get out of here.'

They began to shuffle forward again, Nuala alert now to every lump in the rock. Her whole body tensed, expecting at every moment to feel a lump turn into a snake which would suddenly writhe and twist beneath her feet, biting at her ankles.

Then the tunnel widened out and the roof rose still more and they found themselves in a small cavern. Standing at last beside Kevin and Amanda, Nuala could finally see for herself the crevice ahead of them. A narrow beam of sunlight shone like a torch on the floor, leaving the sides of the cavern in blackness.

Still thinking about snakes, Nuala hurried eagerly towards the light. Then she became aware of a rustling sound. It was coming from one of the unlit corners of the cave, slightly ahead of her and to her right. She stopped dead, seeing in her mind's eye a great snake uncoiling itself and slithering across the rocky floor towards her.

Staring in the direction from which the sound had come, she spied a shadowy figure emerging from the blackness.

For a second Nuala felt relief. Anybody, no matter who it was, was preferable to a snake. Then the light from the crevice shone full on the figure and a scream burst from her. The face was so thin and bony it looked like a skull. It wore a shapeless garment like a shroud and held a long wooden stick in its hand ending in a metal blade with a strange sort of gadget attached.

As Nuala stared in horror, the figure raised the stick in a gesture that was half-appealing, half-menacing. Shrinking away from it towards the opposite side of the cave, Nuala felt something shifting beneath her feet. She screamed again and tried to pull her feet clear of the things which clung to them, but tripped and fell to the ground.

CHAPTER 5

Snakes Alive!

Instead of the rocky floor of the cave, Nuala found she was sprawled on top of something soft, slippery and shifting. With another scream she struggled to her feet, managed to drag her ankles clear of whatever it was that clung to them and ran as fast as she could towards the cleft in the rock. Nor did she stop running until she found herself out on the open mountainside.

Blood trickled down her arm, where she had scraped it against the wall of the cave, but she never even noticed. The creepers outside seemed to trail their fronds everywhere on purpose to trip her, but she just kept running. All she could think of was to put as much distance as possible between herself and the sinister figure in the cave. Only when she was a good distance from the mouth of the cave did she remember Kevin and Amanda. She turned back in time to see them climbing through the gap after her.

'Quick!' she called, 'in case he comes after us!'

'He won't,' Kevin said reassuringly. 'He vanished when you screamed.'

'I reckon he was as scared of us as we were of him,' Amanda agreed. 'He disappeared right back into the darkness again.'

'He looked like a ghost!' Nuala panted.

'With a skull instead of a head!' Kevin agreed.

'And did you get a load of that thing in his hand?' Amanda asked. 'It was the dead spit of the thing Poppa says the Incas used for ploughing the terraces. He showed me a picture of one in his book.'

Kevin gaped at Amanda open-mouthed. 'The ghosts of his ancestors,' he muttered.

'Huh?' Amanda stared back at him. 'What?'

'The old man on the train from Cuzco,' Kevin explained. 'He warned me not to climb Huayna Picchu. If I did I'd be sorry, he said. The ghosts of his ancestors would be angry.'

'You think that was the g-g-ghost of an Inca?' Nuala stammered.

'Aw, come on, you guys!' Amanda protested. 'That's way out!'

'I'm only telling you what he said,' Kevin told her.

'You're just joking, aren't you?' Amanda said, but even *she* sounded uncertain.

'Come on,' Nuala cried, 'let's get out of here!' And forgetting about snakes, she began to slither and slide her way down the faint track leading from the opening in the cliff face, as fast as her feet would take her.

'Hey!' Amanda called. 'Slow down! That track's steep!'

But Nuala didn't seem to hear her. Fuelled by fear, she fled like a frightened mare, her flying feet barely touching the ground. Suddenly the track veered sharply to the right. Unable to slow for the turn, Nuala grabbed a large rock ahead of her, as her feet started to go from under her. Looking down, she cried out in terror. Beyond the rock was a sheer drop of about a hundred feet. If the rock hadn't brought her up sharp, Nuala would have plunged straight over it.

'Snakes alive!' Amanda cried, as she reached her side. 'You coulda broken your neck!'

Nuala, who had been staring as if hypnotised at the drop below, suddenly came to life again.

'Snakes!' she yelled. 'That's what I fell on in the cave! Hundreds of them!'

'Baloney!' Amanda snapped. 'Get a hold of yourself! This is no place for hysterics!'

'But it's true!' Nuala shouted. 'I could feel them wriggling under me!'

'Okay, if you say so,' Amanda said, 'but calm down. It's real dangerous to panic on a mountain.'

'Why don't you believe me?' Nuala almost sobbed. 'They were winding themselves around my ankles!'

'Right!' Amanda retorted. 'But they didn't bite, or hiss or rattle! You sure are lucky in the snakes you get to fall on!'

'They were horrible!' Nuala cried. 'All cold and slithery!'

'Then they weren't snakes,' Kevin told her, as he caught up with them. 'Snakes aren't cold. They look like they ought to be but they're not. Remember when the keeper put one round my neck? On my tenth birthday, in the zoo? You were too scared to let him put it round you. If you had you'd know. Snakes feel warm and cuddly!'

'I wouldn't suggest cuddling up to any around these parts,' Amanda said dryly. 'Poppa says if they bite you, you gotta get an injection real fast. They do feel warm to touch, though, so whatever it was Nuala fell on it sure as hell wasn't a pile of live snakes!'

'Maybe they were dead snakes so,' Kevin teased. 'She must have found a snakes' cemetery!'

'It's not funny!' Nuala snapped. 'And you wouldn't be so smart if it had been *you* who'd fallen on them!'

'Cool it!' Amanda told her. 'You gotta go easy up here. No panicking, no running and no fighting. And you lay off her, Kevin!'

'Okay,' Kevin agreed, 'but she does ask for it. Look at her! Staring like a loony with her hair full of leaves.'

Nuala ran her fingers angrily through her hair and looked at the leaves she found in her hand. Dull green in colour but with a shiny surface, they were about two inches long and shaped like an egg.

'I don't know how *they* got there,' she muttered.

'I guess if you charge down the mountain like a bulldozer you get to scoop up dead leaves,' Amanda said. 'Or maybe they blew into the cave and you collected them when you fell.'

'Maybe *that's* what you fell on,' Kevin suggested. 'A pile of dead leaves someone used for bedding.'

'Except that they're not dead,' Nuala pointed out. 'Look at how shiny they are! They must be off a bush or a tree that's still growing.'

'Yeah,' Amanda agreed, 'you got something there. I reckon they came off one of those shrubs up there.'

Nuala turned and saw she was pointing back up the mountain. A little way above the cave, the whole mountainside was covered with bushes of exactly the same green as the leaves in her hand.

'I think that must be a tea plantation,' she said 'like the one Mum said was on the other side of the valley.'

'So tea *is* grown on Huayna Picchu after all,' Kevin commented.

Nuala sniffed at the leaves and wrinkled her nose. 'They don't smell a bit like tea,' she said.

'That's because they have to be dried first, stupid,' Kevin told her.

'Then I'll try keeping them till they dry,' Nuala said, stuffing them into the pockets of her jeans.

She was turning away when Kevin's words stopped her.

'Hey!' he said suddenly. 'That's funny!' He was still staring at the slope of mountain running up above the cave towards the peak. Nuala could see nothing peculiar about it.

'What is?' she asked.

'The track. You can hardly see the bit we just came down, but higher up it's as clear as anything.'

Then Nuala saw what he meant. There was a well-marked path leading directly from the mouth of the cave to the rows of bushes.

'It must be to do with the plantation,' she said.

'Hey guys,' Amanda cried impatiently, 'are we gonna stand around here all day arguing or are we gonna try and make the dig before they pack up for the night?'

'Where *is* the dig anyway?' Kevin asked, turning back to peer cautiously over the rock at the drop below.

'Down there some place,' Amanda told him. 'I guess we just follow the track.'

The three of them slowly descended the side of Huayna Picchu that was never shown in the guide books and travel books. The track wound its way tortuously amongst rocks and shrubs. Nuala took it more slowly now as she followed Kevin.

They walked in silence, needing all their concentration to keep their footing. Nuala had thought going down would be much easier than going up but, though it was less tiring, the descent was definitely more— dangerous. The track up the other side of the mountain had been bad, but at least it was clearly marked. On this side it seemed to be so rarely used that creepers trailed across it everywhere, hiding the track and catching at their feet to trip them.

Gradually the track, so alarmingly steep for the first fifty feet or so, turned diagonally across the mountain down in the direction of the shoulder. The going became easier and Nuala began to relax a little and look about her. With the sun beating down out of a clear blue sky and the purple mountain range stretching into the hazy distance, the thought of ghosts seemed childish and she felt ashamed of her earlier terror. Could they really have seen that skeletal figure in the shroud-like garment, holding an ancient plough as if it were Death's scythe?

As for snakes, she had to admit that Kevin's explanation made sense. She could hardly have fallen on a bed of snakes and remained unbitten. But what animal would lie on a bed of leaves in such a cave? This was no Irish mountain grazed by sheep or goats, and even the alpaca seemed to remain on the lower slopes. What animal would sleep in such a place? Only then did she remember that Amanda had mentioned bears. Could she have blundered, like Goldilocks, into the home of the three bears? But these would be no porridge-eating teddies. She shivered at the image of a great grizzly who would never wait to ask who had been sleeping in *his* bed. There might have been something more dangerous than a ghost awaiting them. She opened her mouth to tell Amanda this but thought better of it. She would only laugh at her. Amanda was always so cool.

At that moment Amanda screamed. She had stopped abruptly on the track ahead of Kevin, one foot raised and her whole body frozen as if she were playing 'Grandmother's Steps', 'Statues', or 'What's the Time, Mr Wolf'! Then she stepped back heavily on top of Kevin.

'Hey! Will you look where you're putting your big feet!' Kevin protested.

'What's wrong?' Nuala asked, for Amanda looked anything but cool now, clinging on to Kevin as if she was the one seeing ghosts.

For once Amanda appeared speechless. She pointed dumbly at a dry stick lying across the path in front of her, in the middle of a little clear patch.

'What is it?' Kevin asked, stooping to peer at the stick.

'Don't touch it!' Amanda yelled, suddenly finding her voice again.

As she did so, the 'stick' moved by itself, slowly sliding away into the creeper beside the track with a dry rustling sound.

'What was it?' Nuala asked.

'Whaddya think?' Amanda asked back. 'After all your talk, when you actually *see* a snake you don't recognise it. It must have been sunning itself on the track.'

'And you nearly stood on it!' Nuala gasped. 'Would it have killed you?'

'I reckon it would have done its best,' Amanda grinned. She seemed to have completely recovered her cool. 'Snakes don't like being walked on, any more than most folks do. And you don't find injections of anti-snake venom sitting on the sides of mountains like fire-extinguishers on the Empire State Building!'

'Wow!' Nuala breathed. 'And I was just thinking that now it wasn't so steep I didn't need to watch my feet all the time.'

'I guess you can never really relax up here,' Amanda said, as she set off once more.

From then on, Nuala kept her head down, inspecting every trailing frond ahead of her before stepping on it. They continued on until Amanda, still leading the way, suddenly stopped and put her finger to her lips. She pointed below them to their right, where the track ran gently over the shoulder of the mountain and into a valley. A herd of deer was grazing peacefully along its slope. At their head stood a great stag. As they watched, hardly daring to breathe, he suddenly raised his antlered head, turning it and sniffing the air as if he knew there were strangers about.

'He can smell us!' Nuala whispered.

But the stag wasn't looking towards them. He was looking towards the mountain peak behind them. There was a sudden loud crack of a rifle and the stag, followed by the whole herd, raced off around the side of the slope, bouncing in a series of great leaps, until they were out of sight.

'Oh, how could they shoot at the deer!' Nuala cried, as the sound of the shot echoed around the mountains, but again Amanda silenced her, pointing urgently back towards the peak.

Now Nuala could see that there were people in amongst the shiny green bushes high up on the mountain above the cave. They were quite a distance away, but she could see that there were two distinct groups of people. One group had baskets slung on their backs and were standing dotted about among the bushes. The other group, of five men, stood almost in a line on the track, except for one man who was standing a little ahead of the rest.

As she watched, he made a small gesture with his hand, as if pushing his hair back out of his eyes. Then Nuala noticed that he and his four companions were all holding guns.

'What's going on?' she whispered.

'Can't you see?' Kevin muttered. 'They're going to shoot the others!'

'What!' Nuala gasped. 'We must stop them!'

'We can't,' Amanda warned her, 'and if we don't keep quiet they'll get us too!'

CHAPTER 6

The Pay-off

Nuala looked at Amanda in horror. 'But we can't just stand here and watch!' she protested.

'For crying out loud, d'you want them to hear you?' Amanda hissed back. 'If they know we've seen them, they'll come down after us!'

Nuala stood rigid, her fingers in her ears, waiting for the burst of gunfire to echo around the valley. Then all the bright-coloured blobs, that were people with mothers and fathers or sons and daughters, would drop to the ground and lie with sightless eyes looking up at that bright blue sky.

She couldn't bear to watch and yet she couldn't look away. It was like all the times when she was little and she had been unable to look away from the violent films Kevin had watched on telly, but had crouched in a corner, praying for them to end, her eyes glued to the screen. But this wasn't a film. This was real.

Then the five men lowered their guns. One of the

coloured blobs was moving towards the men, his hand outstretched. As he got closer, the man standing out in front limped forward to meet him and took whatever was being held out to him. Then the man with the limp shouted out something and the armed men all turned away and began moving off down the track.

'They're coming this way!' Nuala gasped.

She looked around for a hiding place, but there was nothing but a large overhanging rock about twenty feet below.

'Are you mad?' Amanda croaked in a hoarse whisper, as she saw Nuala measuring the distance with her eyes. 'You'd never make it!'

'Hang on,' Kevin whispered, gripping Nuala's arm. 'They're not coming this way after all.'

The men with guns had reached the bottom of the shiny green patch and were turning to their left along the line of the bushes, following the man with the limp. They watched until the last one had disappeared in the direction of the slope where the deer had been grazing.

'Thank goodness!' breathed Nuala.

Even Kevin still spoke in a hushed voice, though the armed men had gone. Now the rest of the bright coloured blobs were once more hardly visible as they stooped amongst the bushes.

'You can say *that* again!' he muttered.

'But why didn't they shoot?' Nuala asked, raising her voice above a whisper for the first time since she had seen the gunmen.

'Because the man gave them something,' Kevin told her.

'Yeah, I reckon he bought them off,' Amanda agreed. 'Otherwise they'd have been wiped out.'

'Like José's brother,' Nuala said.

Amanda looked at her in surprise.

'D'you mean José who works in the dining-room?' she asked.

Kevin glared at Nuala. 'His brother was killed yesterday,' he told Amanda reluctantly. 'They found his body this morning, but we don't know if he was shot.'

'I don't think he was,' Nuala said. 'I never heard any gunfire before he cried out, but I bet it was those men that killed him.'

'I thought you said the cry you heard was a condor,' Amanda told her indignantly. 'You said nothing about José's brother.'

'We were afraid your mother wouldn't let you come if she knew,' Kevin admitted, 'and we'd never have found the way by ourselves.'

'And you wouldn't trust me not to tell her, you miserable jerks!' Amanda cried. 'That's the last time I do anything for you!'

She flounced off ahead of them down the track.

'You couldn't keep your big mouth shut, could you?' Kevin hissed at Nuala, as the two of them followed her. 'She'll be a pain for the rest of the day now.'

After about ten minutes the track ran over the shoulder of Huayna Picchu and began curving back to the left. Now they were moving towards the base of the sheer cliff over which Nuala had so nearly fallen. Suddenly Amanda stopped and pointed.

'There's the dig down there,' she said, 'and that cave must be the Temple of the Moon.'

She was pointing at a dark opening in the cliff face. It was not unlike the cave mouth they had emerged from almost an hour ago. Below it stretched a small plateau from which the ground fell away steeply to the valley far beneath. Nuala thought it had the same look as Machu Picchu – like a dish, suspended in space.

'It's another flying saucer,' she cried, 'only smaller.'

'It looks like an ordinary cave to me,' Kevin muttered and then, before Nuala could explain what she meant, 'Hey! There's the jeep!'

Then Nuala saw it too, like a toy car parked on the edge of the plateau, a tarpaulin stretched over the bonnet to shield it from the heat. She supposed there had to be a track somewhere leading up from the valley, just as there was at Machu Picchu, though she couldn't see it. From where they stood it looked as if only a helicopter could land on the small flat space in front of the cave. Now she could see two ant-like figures moving around inside a square patch where the vegetation had been cut away.

'One of them must be Mum,' Kevin said. 'Come on. My tongue's as dry as a bone and they'll have something to drink down there.'

Now that their journey was nearly at an end, Nuala

forgot all about snakes. She hurried down until she was close enough to recognise the tiny figure of her mother. Dressed in her overalls, she was squatting on her hunkers, digging with a small trowel inside the patch where the creepers had been cleared. Cupping her hands to her mouth, Nuala shouted as loudly as she could: 'Hi, Mum! Coo-ee!'

Her mother looked all around her in evident surprise, but could see no-one on the little plateau.

'We're up here!' Nuala yelled.

Her mother turned around, shading her eyes from the sun, and looked up towards the peak of Huayna Picchu. Nuala, Kevin and Amanda were all waving to attract her attention. They laughed as they saw her mouth open wide in surprise. As she called to Amanda's father, pointing up at them, they hurried on down the track to meet her.

'Where are the others?' Amanda muttered. 'I thought there were three or four local men working with them on the dig.'

'Maybe they're inside the Temple of the Moon,' Kevin suggested.

'Give me a break,' Amanda snapped, still smarting at Kevin and Nuala's lack of faith in her, 'they were supposed to be clearing the creepers. They seem to have done awfully little.'

'How the hell did you get here?' her father asked as Amanda strolled over to him, as casually as if she had just stepped out of a car.

'Up Huayna Picchu and through the tunnel,' she shrugged.

'Well I'll be danged!' he cried. 'So it *does* go through!'

'Just like you said!' she answered. 'So, how many palaces have you dug up?'

'None yet,' her father laughed, 'though I reckon we've uncovered the end wall of a house. I'm sure glad I didn't know you were on that mountain. We heard what we thought was gunfire from up there a while back.'

'It *was* gunfire,' Kevin told him, filling a mug from the big plastic water container. 'They were shooting at people. We saw them.'

'You could have been killed!' his mother cried, hurrying over to them. 'Didn't I tell you not to go wandering about on your own while you're here? If you wanted to see the dig, why didn't you ask if you could come with us?'

'But we didn't know about José's brother then,' Nuala explained, flopping down wearily on the ground beside the water container. 'And that's what we came to warn you about.'

'Who's José?' her mother asked, bewildered.

'The waiter,' Kevin told her, gulping down the last of the water. 'His brother's body was found this morning by workers going up to the plantation. They said he was thrown off the mountain and killed. We think it may have been the *Sendero Luminosa* who did it, so we thought we'd better warn you, because it happened so close to the dig.'

'And knowing that, you went up there yourselves!' his mother cried in horror. 'I should never have brought you here!'

'Relax,' Mr Houston told her. 'The plantation's way over on the far side of the valley. I reckon it'd take the best part of two hours to get there from here, except as the condor flies.'

'But it was the plantation on Huayna Picchu,' Nuala corrected him. 'The one right up there!'

And she pointed up towards the eastern slope below the peak.

'My God!' her mother gasped.

'But there's no tea grown on Huayna Picchu,' Mr Houston argued. 'It's too isolated. Transportation costs would make it uneconomic. Across the valley the slope isn't so steep and they can run trucks right up to the plantation for loading. They'd never put a plantation up *there*.'

'That's just where you're wrong, Poppa,' Amanda told him. 'We saw the pickers working the bushes with baskets on their backs.'

'But there's only a rough track up to it,' he objected. 'I can't see how they'd carry the tea down.'

'All the same, the bushes are there,' Kevin said. 'Right where I'm pointing.'

Everyone turned to look up at the eastern slope again. From that distance though, the patch of green could as easily have been cactus or creeper, for the rows of neatly-planted bushes were only a blur. Mr

Houston shook his head in disbelief.

'They'd never plant tea up there,' he said again. 'It's too high up.'

'Well, they did,' Nuala exclaimed, 'and I've the leaves to prove it!' She pulled the leaves from her pocket and waved them triumphantly at Mr Houston. He took them from her and examined them closely.

'Well, I'll be danged!' he declared.

He turned the egg-shaped leaves over in his hand, inspecting the markings on them. Finally he sniffed them.

'And you say you got these up there?' he asked. 'But that's gotta be all of nine thousand feet and tea doesn't grow above six thousand.'

'So now who says there's no tea on Huayna Picchu?' Amanda jeered.

'Look, honey,' Mr Houston said patiently. 'These are no tea leaves you've gotten hold of. This is coca!'

'Coca!' Nuala's mother's jaw dropped. 'The stuff they make cocaine out of?'

'Erythroxolyn Coca, to give it its proper name,' Mr Houston nodded. 'Thought by the Incas to be a symbol of royalty and chewed by the Indians to dull the pangs of hunger.'

'Snakes alive!' Amanda cried. 'We could sell these for a fortune back home! They'll pay any amount of dollars for "coke"!'

'You wouldn't get much "coke" out of two leaves,' Kevin grinned. 'We'd want to go back and pick a few more.'

'You'll do no such thing!' his mother cried indignantly. 'That stuff *kills* people!'

And she looked at the two leaves, lying harmlessly in the palm of Mr Houston's hand, as if they were loaded guns. Kevin laughed at her horror, but Mr Houston looked serious.

'Your mother's right,' he said. 'This is no laughing matter. You kids have gotten yourselves into something bigger than you realise. Now, I want you to think carefully. Did anyone see you near those coca shrubs?'

'Nobody except the ghost,' Nuala said. 'Though I don't think he was a *real* ghost. He just appeared so suddenly out of the dark.'

'And he had one of those Chaki-things you said the Incas used for ploughing,' Kevin added.

'A *chaqui-tacllá*,' Mr Houston nodded. 'Yeah, they still use them today on the steeper slopes.'

'And his eyes were sunk right into his head and his bones stuck out like a skeleton,' Amanda finished.

'Sounds like the symptoms of cocaine addiction,' Mr Houston told her. 'Where exactly did you see this guy?'

'In the cave,' Kevin said. 'Nuala was so scared of him that she ran, but she fell over onto a pile of old leaves or something, but she thought they were snakes and ...'

'Leaves?' Mr Houston interrupted. 'She fell on *leaves?*'

'I didn't think they were leaves then because they were sort of slippery,' Nuala told him, 'And they seemed to cling to me like they were alive, but I think now they must have been leaves and that that's how I got the two

I gave you, because they were sort of caught up in my hair and –'

'And was this ghost-guy there when you fell?' Mr Houston interrupted. He seemed to be getting more and more concerned.

'That's why I fell,' Nuala nodded, 'because he gave me such a fright. And I started to run and tripped.'

'So that at least one of these guys saw you right by the coca!' Mr Houston exclaimed.

'Ah, no,' Nuala explained patiently. 'The coca bushes were way up above the cave and I ran straight down. Then the others came after me to try and stop me running in case I'd fall again. We didn't see the bushes till Amanda noticed the leaves in my hair and we wondered where they'd come from. That's when Amanda spotted the bushes higher up the mountain.'

'So we never got to see the bushes close up,' Amanda concluded.

But Mr Houston, who was always so cool and easy-going, suddenly exploded.

'You crazy dumb kids!' he shouted. 'You *still* don't get it, do you? You walked right into the place where they store the coca!'

Everyone looked at him.

'Huh?' Kevin muttered.

'It explains how they solve their transport problem,' Mr Houston continued. 'They must store the coca leaves in the cave until they dry out. With the moisture out of them they'd be a lot lighter and take up a lot less space.

And of course they don't need the same quantities of coca for shipment as they would tea. I guess they just carry it down on their backs when it's dry. And you stumbled right into their secret hideout!'

Nuala noticed that her mother had gone very white.

'D'you think someone might come after them?' she whispered.

'Let's hope not,' Mr Houston told her. 'But I wouldn't bet my last dollar on it. I guess by now the word must have gone around and potential informers are bound to be bad news. From now on the kids would wanna stay close to the hotel or travel with a bunch of tourists. I figure they could be in real danger.'

CHAPTER 7

The Unexpected Visitor

'They wouldn't come looking for them here, would they?'

Kevin could hear the fear in his mother's voice. 'Of course not,' he said confidently. 'If we stick around the dig or the hotel we'll be fine.'

'I hope for all our sakes that you're right,' Mr Houston said, 'but it depends on who we're dealing with here. I reckon we won't have too much trouble from the locals. The Quechua-speaking Amerindians are a fine race, directly descended from the Incas. They've suffered persecution and discrimination since the Spanish conquest and sometimes this has driven them to violence, but they're a gentle people under normal circumstances.'

'What about the men with guns?' Nuala asked. 'The ones we saw up there. D'you think they belong to the *Sendero Luminosa*?'

'I guess they could, but I sure hope they don't,' Mr Houston said. 'They haven't been operating around here for the past few years, though in 1986 they bombed the tourist train from Cuzco, and killed seven people. They all but wiped out the tourist trade in Machu Picchu for a couple of years. If it was the *Sendero* you saw I just hope they didn't see you!'

'What exactly *did* you see?' her mother asked Nuala anxiously.

'We heard a bang,' Nuala said, 'and we thought someone was shooting at the deer ...'

'You mean, *you* did,' Kevin cut in, 'but I saw these men with their guns pointed at the people in amongst the bushes.'

'The ones with the baskets on their backs,' Nuala added.

'Can you describe these gunmen?' Mr Houston asked.

'They looked just the same as the pickers,' Kevin told him, 'in big loose shirts.'

'But they had the drop on the pickers,' Amanda added, 'and I reckon they would have shot them, only one of the other guys gave them something and they split.'

'Sounds like they were being bought off,' Mr Houston commented.

'D'you think the *Sendero Luminosa* takes a rake-off from the cocaine trade, like the Mafia?' Kevin's mother suggested.

'I'd be surprised,' Mr Houston said. 'Oh, they're a ruthless bunch, I grant you. They've murdered more than twenty-three thousand people since they were founded in 1980, and committed some real gruesome atrocities. They've attacked missionaries and even nuns – apparently on the grounds that the missions are delaying the revolution by helping the people so they're less likely to revolt.'

'So I don't see why you think they'd stop at profiting by the drug trade,' Kevin's mother said.

'I guess they haven't too many scruples,' Mr Houston agreed, 'but in their own strange way they're idealists. They believe they're acting in the interest of the people. They believe everything they're doing is serving the revolution, and I don't figure they'd rob their own people.'

'But supposing they needed money to buy arms,' Kevin's mother argued. 'Mightn't they decide the end justified the means?'

'Could be,' Mr Houston said. 'It sure would explain why Jorge and the others fled the minute they heard the firing.'

'So *that's* what happened to them!' Amanda exclaimed. 'I was trying to figure how come you two got to be working here on your own.'

'Yeah, and by the same token it's time we got back down to it,' Mr Houston commented. 'Unless we want some other guy getting the credit for the discovery of Machu Marca. We've less than three months to complete the job and, if your theory is correct, we may have trouble recruiting more local help.'

'Can we not drop the kids back to the hotel first?' Kevin's mother pleaded.

Mr Houston shook his head. 'By the time we got back here there'd be less than an hour's daylight left,' he said. 'They can stay out of sight in the Temple of the Moon.'

'Give us a break!' Amanda snapped. 'If you think I'm gonna spend hours skulking in there you've another think coming! I've had enough of caves for one day.'

'Now, honey –' her father began, but Nuala cut in on him.

'Why don't we pretend to be helpers?' she suggested. 'If we put on overalls no-one would ever know from a distance we weren't local people.'

'Yeah,' Kevin agreed. 'We could cut back the creeper for you.'

'You did say you needed help,' Nuala added.

'I'd be scared you'd cut yourselves,' her mother replied. 'Those machetes are really sharp.'

'You must think we're real dumb!' Amanda cried indignantly.

'We'll be careful, Mum,' Nuala promised. 'Honest!'

'What d'you think, Chuck?' her mother asked Mr Houston.

'I guess if they're dead careful they could give it a try,' he replied. 'But you kids won't find it as easy as you think. You'd want to take it real slow till you get the hang of it.'

So it was that ten minutes later, wearing overalls and armed with machetes, the three new recruits were ready to begin work.

'Just let anyone from the *Sendero Luminosa* come near

me and I won't be long chopping his head off!' Kevin joked, flourishing his machete.

'That's just the sort of stupid behaviour we *don't* want,' his mother told him. 'Don't wave that blade around or we'll have an accident.'

'I guess it would be wise to have them start chopping in different places,' Mr Houston agreed. 'That way they'd only have to take care not to hack their own limbs by mistake.'

So they were each taken to different corners of the site and shown how to clear away the creeper which had spread everywhere in tangled heaps over the ground in front of the temple. For a while they worked away in silence, for cutting through the tough fronds was decidedly tricky. Though the machete was dangerously sharp, Kevin found the muscles in his arms soon began to ache from the unfamiliar movement needed to avoid swinging the blade towards himself. He was therefore only too glad when a shout from his mother gave him the excuse to stop for a while.

'What is it?' he asked, going over to where she had been digging with her trowel, beside the stones Mr Houston had described as possibly the end wall of a house.

'This wall is circular!' she shouted excitedly. 'Maybe it's like the one in Huinay Huayna.'

When Kevin had glanced at it earlier, without much interest, it had consisted of half-a-dozen large smooth stones placed two-deep on top of each other in the same way as those in the walls of Machu Picchu. Now he could see that, although there were only another four or five stones visible, the wall was following an unmistakable curve.

'It might just be a round building,' he said. 'I mean, the Temple of the Sun at Machu Picchu looked like a Martello tower!'

'I suppose you could say that, to the extent that both are circular,' Mr Houston said sarcastically. 'Apart from that, they're pretty different.'

'But wouldn't it be wonderful if this turned out to pre-date the Incas?' Kevin's mother cried. 'After all, the buildings at Gran Vilaya are mostly circular and the ones at Huaca are U-shaped, and they're both much earlier sites than Machu Picchu.'

'Yeah, but both sites are over to the north-west,' Mr Houston told her. 'There's been nothing from the early civilisations found anywhere near here.'

'That's what would make it so exciting,' Kevin's mother said. 'It would prove that the early coastal tribes moved much further inland than has been supposed up to this. And you have always suspected that this site might be earlier than Machu Picchu. Isn't that why you provisionally named it Machu Marca, the "old city"?'

'I guess we're just gonna have to wait and see,' Mr Houston laughed. 'We're gonna have to do a lot more digging before we can even speculate.'

So, after he had had another go at the water container, Kevin went back to the cutting. By the time Mr Houston finally called a halt to the day's work, they were all exhausted, even though, to Nuala's disgust, Amanda appeared as cool as ever.

Surveying the work they had done, Nuala had to admit that they had made very little impression on the creeper. There was so much of it and the plateau which had looked so small from above seemed a great deal larger now. The ground was also less flat than she had supposed. Everywhere there were mounds and hillocks, lumps and bumps and she began to share her mother's excitement as to what might lie beneath them. She had almost forgotten the dangers that threatened them until her mother spoke again.

'Hurry up and get into the jeep,' she said, after they had taken off their overalls and lifted the empty water container into the back. 'I won't rest easy until you're all safely back at the hotel.'

It was a long and bumpy journey, for there was no proper track leading down from the mountain on this side. They drove along a rutted footpath little better than the one they had followed down from the upper cave, although it was much less steep. Following a long diagonal route to the far-off valley, it would have made for easy walking, but would have taken them many hours.

The jeep pitched and rolled like a small boat in heavy seas and often Nuala suspected that not all four wheels were on the ground. By the time they reached the main road she felt battered as well as exhausted and hardly glanced at the view of Huayna Picchu towering above them, even when Kevin commented: 'We were right up there a few hours ago!'

When they got back to the hotel, Kevin's mind was fixed on getting a coke, while Nuala longed for a bath.

'I think we should all have baths now,' her mother agreed. 'Judging by yesterday, it's the only time of day that the water's really hot. Then we can all meet for a drink before dinner.'

'I just gotta have me a beer before I drag myself upstairs,' Mr Houston said apologetically. 'I'll stay here with Kevin and follow you up later. We won't be long,' he promised.

As it turned out, however, he was wrong.

Mrs Houston was already in the lounge, and Kevin and her husband joined her, collapsing wearily into chairs on either side of her.

'Where's Amanda?' she asked Kevin anxiously. 'I thought she was with you.'

'She's gone for a bath,' Kevin told her. 'She'll be here soon.'

'Not that young lady!' her mother grinned. 'When Amanda takes a bath, she likes to take her time too. But you might have told me this morning where you were going.'

'I'm sorry Mrs Houston,' Kevin apologised, 'but Nuala and I only decided to go at the last minute, and Amanda came with us to show us the way.'

'I guess it's no good blaming you,' Mrs Houston

admitted. 'Amanda's big and bold enough to tell me herself. I was real worried about her until I met that young couple from Ohio. They told me they saw the three of you setting out to climb Huayna Picchu.'

'I suppose Amanda forgot,' Kevin said. 'She was in a hurry to get us packed lunches at the last minute.'

'Well, she'd no darn business forgetting,' Mrs Houston grumbled. 'And you were gone for so long. It's a pretty long climb, I guess, but when I heard the military were out and about I got worried again.'

'The military!' Mr Houston echoed. 'Now what would bring them up here?'

'Don't ask me!' his wife exclaimed. 'But when I saw that Ohio couple off to the bus for Puente Ruinas the driver said there were soldiers down at the station.'

'I guess they got word that guerrillas had been seen around the place,' Mr Houston said. 'That oughta be reassuring but I reckon soldiers swarming around the dig asking questions might be near as bad as the guerrillas. Did the driver say *why* they were here?'

'He just kept right on complaining about them harassing the stall-holders in Puente Ruinas,' Mrs Houston told him. 'What's all that about guerrillas?'

Mr Houston darted a warning glance at Kevin. 'There was a rumour they'd been seen on Huayna Picchu,' he said.

'Then I suggest you tell that daughter of ours to stay away from it,' Mrs Houston ordered.

'I already have, honey,' Mr Houston reassured her.

'Whaddya think's happened those drinks? I ordered them at least ten minutes back.'

'I guess there's your answer?' Mrs Houston replied, looking over in the direction of the bar. 'The waiter's vanished!'

It was at that moment that the hotel manager came into the lounge. Kevin recognised him immediately because he had seen him the evening before when Mr Houston had introduced him. The manager had told his mother, in a heavily-accented voice, that he hoped she would be comfortable during her three-month stay: he had given her their very best room. Kevin had remarked afterwards that, if *that* was their best room, he wouldn't like to have to stay in their *worst*, but his mother had been annoyed.

'It's clean and comfortable, even if it is a bit shabby,' she had snapped. 'This isn't a luxury hotel for long-stay holidaymakers. The rooms are just for people to stay overnight in and I see absolutely nothing wrong with it.'

Kevin had felt at the time that the manager seemed pretty laid back and unlikely to be too worried about what his mother thought of the room, but he looked anything but laid back now. He stood just inside the door, nervously tapping the fingers of one hand on the bar counter and looking anxiously around the room as he tried to get everyone's attention.

'Ladies and gentlemen,' he began, without much effect. Then, raising his voice to an almost hysterical pitch: '*Ladies and gentlemen, please! I beg you ...!*'

Heads turned, chairs were pushed back and gradually the hum of conversation and the clink of glasses died away.

'Thank you, ladies and gentlemen, for your attention,' the manager continued. 'I must ask you please to remain here for the time being. I have asked that all guests gather here as soon as possible, so you may hear an important message. Thank you.'

Then, as the buzz of speculation began, he left the room again.

'It's no use his asking Mum and Nuala,' Kevin said. 'I bet they're in the bath by now.'

'I wouldn't put it past that guy to get them out of it,' Mrs Houston said. 'He sounded like he meant business.'

'I'd describe him more as desperate,' her husband said. 'In fact, I'd say he looked dead scared.'

Nuala lay back in the bath, her eyes closed. Despite what her mother had said, the water wasn't very hot, more like lukewarm really, but Nuala was so hot herself she didn't mind a bit. She had dissolved some of her mother's bath salts in it and now, with the business of washing over, she was letting the ache in her limbs dissolve along with the salts.

She wished she didn't have to get out of the bath so soon and get dressed again. It was a long time since she had eaten her chicken sandwiches, but she was too tired even to feel hungry. She felt her head falling forwards and jerked herself up in the bath for fear of getting her hair wet. Then she heard hammering on the bathroom door and her mother's voice calling her name.

'I'm just coming,' she said drowsily.

'Then hurry,' her mother's voice called from behind the door. 'We've to go downstairs right away.'

'It's not that late, is it?' Nuala asked.

'No, but the manager wants to talk to us all,' her mother answered.

Groaning, Nuala tumbled out of the bath and dried herself as quickly as she could. Then she threw on her dressing-gown and ran into the bedroom. Her mother had laid out fresh clothes on her bed and she flung them on as fast as she could. What was all the fuss about? she wondered. Maybe the hotel was on fire? But no, she would have heard some sort of alarm bell. And she would have expected to hear the sounds of running feet and shouting, or smell smoke or hear the crackling of flames. It had to be something a good deal less urgent, and she resented having to cut her bath short.

When she was dressed, she grabbed her hair brush and stood in front of the small mirror by the window, trying to get the tangles out of her hair. She heard the sound of a car pulling up outside, a door slamming and a confident male voice. Glancing out she saw a man in uniform standing beside a car directly below her window.

The uniform he was wearing was not like an Irish army uniform, but she could tell from the braid on it and the decorations on his shoulder that he must be some sort of an officer. In fact, from the deferential way the hotel manager was treating him, Nuala figured he must be someone very important.

As he swept the manager impatiently aside and began to walk towards the hotel door, Nuala caught her breath. Of course, it was not unusual for soldiers to have been wounded and why not in the leg? Yet it seemed a strange coincidence that, that very afternoon, she had seen a man limping in exactly the same way. Of course, he had been a long way away from her but even so ... Then, just as he reached the door, the man made a small gesture, as if he were brushing the hair back from his face.

CHAPTER 8

The Real Picture

Nuala ran quickly into her mother's room. 'That was quick!' her mother said approvingly, dusting her face with powder, 'and I'm just ready too. I wonder what all this is about.'

'We mustn't go down, Mum,' Nuala cried. 'They might shoot us all!'

'Don't be ridiculous,' her mother said. 'It's the manager who wants to talk to us, not the *Sendero Luminosa*.'

'But I saw him!' Nuala exclaimed, clutching her mother's arm.

Her mother stared at her in bewilderment.

'Saw *whom*?' she asked.

'The man who was going to shoot all those people on the mountain!' Nuala shouted. 'I saw him just now from the window, going into the hotel. He's downstairs now, waiting for us!'

'You must have made a mistake,' her mother said, giving a final pat to her hair. 'Maybe it was someone who looked a bit like him.'

'No, Mum, honest. He was in uniform and the manager must be on his side because he was bowing and scraping to him like anything!'

'Really, darling, I don't imagine the hotel manager is in league with a guerrilla. He sounds like some kind of official. Come on, we must go.'

'Oh, Mum, why don't you believe me?' Nuala wailed. 'You'll be sorry when something awful happens.'

'Nothing awful's going to happen,' her mother laughed. 'Honestly, you are extraordinary. Gallivanting about a mountain crawling with drug smugglers and robbers, frightening the life out of me, and you want to know what I'm fussing about! Then the manager wants to say a few words and you become hysterical.'

'I'm not hysterical,' Nuala protested indignantly, 'but I *know* that man's dangerous.'

'Then we'd better go down and make sure Kevin's all right, hadn't we?' her mother asked, walking out of the room.

In desperation Nuala followed her mother out on to the landing. There were several people on the stairs, for many of the guests had been changing for dinner when the manager's message had reached them, so Nuala and her mother joined them as they all headed for the lounge. At the bottom of the stairs Nuala hesitated, but the sight of the man in uniform talking to the manager by the reception desk was enough to send her hurrying on into the lounge after her mother. They sat down beside Kevin and the Houstons.

Nuala leaned across to whisper a warning to Kevin, but he was talking to Mrs Houston. She looked around then for Amanda, but she was nowhere to be seen.

Then the manager ushered the man in uniform into the room and Nuala's eyes became glued to the gun, strapped to his side in a shiny leather holster.

The manager struck a spoon several times against the side of an empty glass on the bar counter and this time everyone fell silent immediately, curious to know why they had all been brought together.

'Where's Amanda?' Nuala whispered, but Mrs Houston only shrugged.

'Still in the bath, I guess,' she muttered. 'I can tell you, it takes more than a polite message to get that lady out of her bath in a hurry.'

'Ladies and gentlemen,' the manager was saying, 'we are all here now, I think, yes? So allow me to introduce to you Captain Ramon of our national army.'

'You see,' Nuala's mother whispered to her. 'You were quite wrong.'

But Nuala noticed that Kevin was also examining the two men closely, and staring hard at Captain Ramon. As the captain limped forward and gestured as if to brush his hair back out of his eyes, Nuala heard Kevin gasp. He too had noticed the resemblance between this smartly-dressed officer and the man in peasant costume they had seen that afternoon on the mountainside.

'So sorry for the interrupt of your stay here to visit this so great treasure of our national culture,' Captain Ramon began, speaking confidently despite his broken English. 'I will not make big delay for you, but you will please listen carefully to this so important warning.'

Nuala and Kevin exchanged glances. This man was not to be trusted.

'Tomorrow,' he continued, 'you will again visit the great Inca city of Machu Picchu before you must take train to Cuzco. Often tourists who are young and strong will rise early on this last day to climb Huayna Picchu for the so great view at sunrise. So sorry but tomorrow this will not be possible. Our army makes manoeuvre there and for you it would not be safe. Perhaps already you hear the sound of gunfire, yes? So now I say again, you must stay away from this mountain. If anybody ignore this warning, I cannot be responsible for the regrettable accident that might take place.' His speech over, Captain Ramon looked over at the hotel manager.

'And I wish only to ask,' the manager added a little nervously, 'that you pay close attention to the words of Captain Ramon, who speaks only for your good. And also to thank him for speaking and, of course, you for listening.' With that, he escorted the soldier out of the room, and immediately the hum of conversation started up again.

'You see,' Nuala's mother cried, sounding greatly relieved, 'that explains what you saw on the mountain today. The whole thing was just a military exercise.'

'Then why were the men with the guns dressed the same as the pickers?' Kevin asked. 'I don't believe a word he said.'

'I guess all this talk about manoeuvres was just to reassure everybody,' Mrs Houston agreed. 'The army may have gotten word that the *Sendero* are active in the neighbourhood. Captain Ramon was sent to clean them out of it and he wants the tourists out of the way in case there's any shooting.'

'Then he's a bit late in the day,' Nuala said, 'because the shooting's already started. We all heard it today.'

'And Captain Ramon admitted it just now,' her mother pointed out. 'I must say I'm happier now the army's here. The thought of guerrillas on Huayna Picchu had me scared stiff.'

'But it was Captain Ramon and his men who were on Huayna Picchu,' Nuala cried. 'You said I only imagined it was him we saw, but Kevin recognised him too, didn't you, Kevin?'

'It was him all right,' Kevin said. 'So what was he doing dressed as a peasant?'

'Maybe the soldiers were disguised in order to infiltrate the guerrillas?' his mother suggested.

'But they weren't guerrillas,' Nuala protested. 'The people they were threatening to shoot were just ordinary farmworkers, except it wasn't tea they were picking.'

'I guess they could have been supporters of the *Sendero*,' Mr Houston said. 'They have a surprising amount of support amongst the peasants. And the army isn't exactly noted for its kid-glove treatment of anyone suspected of helping the guerrillas. That might explain what happened to the brother of that waiter too.'

'Shh!' Nuala whispered, for the barman had appeared again as suddenly as he had disappeared before, bringing the long-awaited drinks.

At that moment Amanda also appeared. She had changed into silk shorts in a pink and lavender floral pattern, with a matching vest top that made Nuala green with envy.

'And where were you, young lady?' her father demanded.

'Changing,' Amanda shrugged, 'and then I met José. I guess I have the real picture now.'   .

'That's the best news I've heard all day,' her mother exclaimed. 'Some of the talk I've been hearing in the past few minutes would drive you to a horror movie for relaxation! So, tell me what's going on, honey!'

'Well, José shut up like a clam when I asked him about the plantation. He was dead scared, I guess, especially when I said we'd seen gunmen on Huayna Picchu. But when I told him we'd seen the coca leaves in the cave and the gunmen threatening the pickers, it loosened his tongue real fast. He says the army are always robbing the people and his brother made up his mind to put a stop to it.'

'So they killed him!' Nuala cried, but Mrs Houston interrupted her.

'Hang on, honey, let's get it from the horse's mouth,'

she said. 'What else did José say, Amanda?'

'His brother called a meeting in Puente Ruinas last week,' Amanda continued, 'and he talked to the people. He told them that the *Sendero* were fighting for the people, not against them, and that their power came from the people; that the rich and the army were the enemies of the revolution, not poor people like them, and that the next time they were asked for money they should tell that to the gunmen and refuse to give them anything.'

'He was a brave man,' Mr Houston commented.

'And look where his courage got him,' his wife interrupted. 'Go on, honey.'

'That's about all, I guess,' Amanda said. 'Then they found his body this morning.'

'And we saw the men that killed him!' Nuala gasped. 'Captain Ramon and his men.'

'Who's Captain Ramon?' Amanda asked.

Kevin told her then about Captain Ramon, his similarity to the armed man on the mountain and the warning he had given.

'So maybe the soldiers were pretending to be from the *Sendero Luminosa* when they robbed the people!' Amanda suggested.

'Don't be ridiculous,' her mother said, but Mr Houston suddenly sat up straight in his chair.

'I guess it's not so ridiculous,' he told her. 'The army in this part of the world has always been pretty powerful. That means governments haven't too much control over what their armies get up to. Some of them have been guilty of really horrific atrocities themselves, if the reports coming back to the US from aid workers are to be believed. To tell you the truth, I reckon there's probably not that much difference between the army and the guerrillas when it comes to violence.'

'But why the heck would they disguise themselves as peasants and threaten to shoot the people?' his wife asked.

'Well, I figure you were right. They were probably sent here to check on reports that the *Sendero* were operating in the area,' Mr Houston answered. 'So they pretended to be from the *Sendero* themselves, in order to find out if there were supporters amongst the people. I guess they reckoned this guy José's brother was at least a sympathiser.'

'But why would they rob the people?' Nuala asked.

'Why not, if they felt like it?' Mr Houston replied. 'There's no one gonna call them to account over it. probably the army haven't gotten a pay rise in a while. Everything here may seem cheap to us, but it's expensive enough for the Peruvians in relation to their pay.'

'But that was real mean!' Nuala cried, 'to rob people who have almost nothing!'

'You forget they're involved in the production of cocaine,' her mother pointed out.

'The peasants don't see it like that,' Mr Houston told her. 'Coca has been grown in Peru since Inca times. It's just another crop to them.'

'Yeah, but the soldiers may have been ordered to try and put a stop to the hard drug trade,' his wife suggested.

'But they didn't!' Kevin argued. 'They only took the profits.'

'And José says the village people don't make a whole lot out of coca anyway,' Amanda added. 'It's the man that *buys* the stuff from them who makes all the money.'

'They're the ones that oughta be behind bars,' her father agreed. 'All the buyers and smugglers and dealers. They're killing people for profit the same as any hired gun. You can't blame the growers. The only way you'd stop the supply at source would be to provide the peasants with some other crop that can be grown high in the mountains and that has guaranteed sales.'

'But if the soldiers are robbing the people we should tell someone!' Nuala exclaimed.

'Like who?' Mr Houston asked. 'I'm afraid the police here are run on pretty much the same lines as the army.'

'Well then, the government,' Nuala cried. 'Surely they'd have to do something?'

'I reckon their chief reaction would be to hush the whole thing up,' Mr Houston told her. 'Anyway, there'll always be someone somewhere who'd think *you* the enemy for attacking the reputation of the national army and decide to hush *you* up!'

'And that's no joke,' Mrs Houston warned. 'You kids had better keep your mouths shut or *you* might be found at the bottom of a ravine like your pal's brother!'

CHAPTER 9

A Quick Change for Amanda

Nuala shuddered.

'But are you saying we can't do a thing about it?' she said.

'Not at all,' Mr Houston told her. 'Once you're safely home you could join Amnesty International. They have members all over the world fighting against the abuse of human rights, which is what this is. They'll advise you how to write to the Peruvian president and to people who have been imprisoned in doubtful circumstances. Governments get worried about what other countries think of them and when they get floods of letters from abroad they have to appear to be doing something. Many prisoners have already been released as a result. It's a slow process, I'm afraid, but it does get results in the end.'

'I'll join the minute I get home,' Nuala cried.

'Me too,' Kevin said. 'And I'll try and get Joe and Jerry to join too.'

Mr Houston nodded. 'And how about you, Amanda?'

'Oh, sure, I'll join,' Amanda told him. 'But that won't do a whole lot for the guys working on the plantation, like Nuala's ghost.'

'For all you know he could be in with the drug smugglers,' her mother pointed out, but Amanda contradicted her.

'Says who? I know all about him. José told me. He's a guy called Juan, who worked alongside José's brother. He's just a peasant, same as the rest of them.'

'Then what was he doing skulking in a cave?' her mother demanded.

'When he heard José's brother had been killed he reckoned he'd be next, so he –' Amanda began, but Kevin interrupted her.

'Hey!' he shouted. 'They're off!'

He was looking past the others out of the long, low window behind them. Turning to peer out, Nuala saw Ramon and his men setting off into the gathering darkness in the direction of Huayna Picchu.

'I'm glad they've gone,' she exclaimed. 'I felt prickly all the time they were around.'

'I reckon they've gone to round up your ghost friend,' Mr Houston told her. 'That's why they want everyone to keep off the mountain.'

'They won't find him in the dark,' Kevin grinned, 'and he could be miles away by morning.'

'I guess that's why they didn't wait for daylight,' Mrs Houston said.

'And I wouldn't be too sure darkness is gonna hide

him. They've pretty powerful flashlights. Look!'

Turning once more, Nuala could see little pools of light beginning to spread out across the ancient city.

'What will they do to him if they find him?' she asked.

Mr Houston looked grave. 'They'll question him,' he said, 'and from all I hear their methods won't be pretty. These lads don't mess around.'

'You mean, they'll torture him?' Kevin asked.

'It seems to be standard practice in these parts,' Mr Houston replied. 'And even if he co-operates, they'll likely throw him into jail and leave him there to rot. Like I said, jails in this part of the world are stuffed full of so-called subversives like your ghost.'

'Oh, I hope he gets away,' Nuala cried.

The others said nothing for a while, thinking of Juan, his skeletal body pressed against the wall in the darkest corner of the cave, while Ramon and his men beat the mountainside in search of him.

Then Amanda broke the silence. 'I say, you guys, are we ever gonna eat? It seems like a hundred years since I ate that scraggy chicken sandwich!'

But even after they had taken their seats in the dining-room they had to wait for what seemed an age before a worried-looking José appeared with their soup.

'Please excuse for the delay,' he muttered, as he put the lukewarm bowls down in front of the three adults, slopping Mrs Houston's slightly as he did so. 'Soldiers search kitchen before they go. Make big mess.'

'He's worried about Juan too,' Amanda whispered, after he had brought her soup without giving her his usual grin.

Dinner continued in its normal slow and uninspired way, yet, although Ramon and his men were long gone, there were to be still more delays.

Moving back to the lounge for coffee, where they found the curtains were now all drawn, they settled themselves down in their usual corner to wait. Ten minutes passed and then a further ten minutes.

'I guess José's forgotten all about the coffee,' Mrs Houston grumbled.

'I'm afraid he's got more than us on his mind tonight,' Nuala's mother told her. Then she turned to Kevin. 'Will you go and see if you can hurry him up?'

'I'll go,' Amanda said, jumping up quickly before Kevin could stir.

She ran into the kitchen. It was deserted. Then she heard low voices coming from the pantry which led off it.

'José!' she called, pushing open the doorway.

She had just time to glimpse a figure with his back to her, wearing a chef's white overalls, before he whirled around, pushing her clear of the door and kicking it shut behind her. It was 'the ghost' – Juan. She opened her mouth to cry out in surprise but, before she could do so, he had seized her and clapped a bony hand over her mouth. He was surprisingly strong for someone who looked like only skin and bone. As she struggled with him José hurried over, speaking to him in a low voice in Quechuan. The man relaxed his violent grip a little, but he didn't take his hand from her mouth.

'Is all right,' José said to Amanda reassuringly. 'Nothing to be afraid. Juan worry only that you scream and people come. I say to him you not tell he is here. You swear?'

Amanda nodded vigorously, but Juan still hesitated. Finally, after studying her face for a long time with his dark, sunken eyes, he let her go.

'Why ... you ... here?' he asked haltingly. Unlike the waiter, he obviously had very little English.

'José never brought the coffee,' Amanda explained.

'I forget,' José apologised. 'Suddenly Juan comes and I forget. I bring now.'

But just then there was a thunderous banging on the front door. José ran to the window, peered through the slit between the drawn curtains and gestured frantically to Juan.

'Is it Ramon?' Amanda asked, as the two men stood motionless for a second as if paralysed with fear. Then she found herself once more in that bony grip as Juan snatched up a kitchen knife and held it threateningly to her throat.

'Stop! I'm on your side!' Amanda cried hoarsely, trying not to scream for fear it would alarm him more. 'Make him let go of me, José!'

The two men began to argue with renewed urgency in Quechuan. Then José turned to her.

'The soldiers! They surround hotel!' he whispered intensely. 'We think kitchen safe because already they search here. Now they come back. Maybe someone see Juan come. If they find, take us too!'

'They mustn't find him,' Amanda said. 'Only let me go and I'll help you.'

There was more hurried whispering between the men but Juan, a wild look in his eyes, still held the knife to her throat.

'He want you for hostage,' José said, waving his arms despairingly. 'He say with you held in front of him they not shoot. Once he get too far for shooting he let you go.'

'But they've got men spread out all over the mountain!' Amanda cried desperately. 'I can't shield him from all directions! Anyway, that trigger-happy bunch would probably plug him straight through me! I know a better way. Just get him to put that knife down!'

There was more urgent whispering and then, slowly and reluctantly, his eyes fixed on her face, Juan lowered the knife. Amanda could hear the sound of tramping feet, raised voices and banging doors from the far side of the hotel. The soldiers must already be inside the building. There was no time to lose.

'Okay,' she said, beginning to strip off her pink and lavender top as the men stared at her. 'Get him to take off his overalls and put these on. And make it snappy!'

In seconds she had put on his soiled white overalls on top of her bra and pants, as Juan struggled into her shorts and top. Amanda looked at him quizzically.

'A pretty good fit,' she said. 'It's his head that's all wrong. I wish I'd a head scarf. Still, it's dark out and ... I know! If he had Kevin and Nuala with him he'd easily pass for me. Hang on, I'll see if I can get them!'

'Is no time!' José implored, but Amanda had run into the kitchen and opened the service hatch to the dining-room. Through the glass dining-room door opposite she could see into the corner of the lounge where the others were sitting. All of them were looking away from her, their attention fixed on something she couldn't see. Maybe Ramon or some of his men were already in the lounge. She dared not go round to them through the hall. Besides, there was no time.

Just at that moment Kevin turned his head. Amanda waved frantically at him but he seemed not to see her. It was hopeless. She would have to chance smuggling Juan out without him, but then Kevin glanced back again, cautiously, as if not wishing to attract attention. She pointed to him and Nuala, then beckoned urgently.

She saw him turn casually to Nuala and whisper something to her. Then slowly, casually, they slipped through the glass door into the dining-room and moved quickly across to the hatch.

'Quick!' Amanda said. 'Climb through into the kitchen and keep your mouths shut!'

The sound of the search was drawing closer and there was no time to explain. Praying Juan wouldn't start his knife act again with Kevin and Nuala and that they wouldn't question her plan, she pulled them through the hatch and dragged them through the kitchen into the pantry.

'You've to go with Juan,' she whispered to them, pointing to the gaunt figure in the floral culottes. 'To make them think he's me. Go fast before anyone comes. I'm going to see if the coast's clear. Wait till you hear me whistle and then hurry.'

She slipped through the scullery to the back door of the hotel and opened it cautiously. Immediately a flash-light shone in her face as a figure in uniform emerged from the darkness beyond. Ramon had stationed one of his men at the back door. She would have to get him away from it somehow. Forgetting she was no longer dressed to kill, she gave him her most dazzling smile.

He said something to her, but Amanda's Spanish wasn't good enough. Weren't soldiers supposed to say: 'Halt! Who goes there?' And the answer, of course, was 'friend'.

'*Amigo!*' she said, repeating the dazzling smile.

The effect was better than she had dared to hope. With a wolfish look, he put an arm around her and began to lead her towards an outhouse to their right, speaking softly words she couldn't understand.

Amanda was triumphant. Like Tank Girl, she would use her charms to get him out of sight of the door and then give Kevin and Nuala the signal.

'*Si! Si!*' she nodded, hoping that was the right answer.

He tightened his arm around her and led her to the

back of the outhouse, pulling her towards him. As he did so, she gave a piercing wolf whistle, hoping he would mistake it for enthusiasm. From his wolfish grin it was clear that he did and Amanda began to feel a small bit uneasy as she listened anxiously for the sound of the back door. He began to tease her – and then she heard the door so plainly that she was afraid he might hear it too. But all his attention seemed to be focused on her.

She wondered how long she needed to distract him to give the others time to get away. His breath smelled unpleasantly of chilli and she disliked the look in his eyes. She wriggled a little but he only grinned and tightened his grip on her.

Meanwhile, Juan, Kevin and Nuala were struggling up the steep mountain slope away from the hotel. There would have been more cover if they had hugged the bushes running back towards the entrance to the city, but Kevin guessed they must be making for the Inca trail which led to Huinay Huayna.

From what his mother had said about it, it would be difficult for Ramon to capture Juan if he could reach such an inaccessible fortress.

Now, with only the darkness to hide them, silence was essential if they were to avoid attracting attention.

Kevin, his breath rasping in his throat, was finding it harder and harder not to pant loudly. Suddenly his foot slipped on a rock and he fell, dislodging a number of smaller rocks, which clattered down the mountainside. Immediately there was a shout and flashlights picked them out as he scrambled to his feet. Then he heard a voice from below them and away to their left, which he recognised at once as Ramon's.

'Stay where you are!'

Kevin grabbed Juan's arm, afraid he might try to make a run for it while they were still within rifle range, instead of trusting to his disguise. But it was Nuala who started to run.

'Come back, Nuala!' Kevin shouted, but she kept going. She was running diagonally down the slope to their right, away from Ramon. Instinctively she was heading for the cover of the bushes which fringed the entrance to the city.

'Stop!' Ramon yelled, but this only seemed to make Nuala run faster.

From the side of the rocky outcrop across which she was running the mountain fell away in a drop of almost six feet. Barely visible from the hotel in the darkness, from Nuala's position it would have been invisible even in daylight, and she was heading straight for the edge.

Amanda too had begun to panic. Her decoy work had been successful, but the soldier was becoming insistent, trying to kiss her. Freeing herself was proving harder than she had imagined it would be. Disdainful glances which worked for Tank Girl were no help now. Her escape route was blocked by the man's stocky body.

All the shouting brought José and the hotel manager to the back door. Suddenly the manager gripped José's arm in horror, pointing to Nuala. José hesitated only for a second. Then he began to run towards Nuala, trying to cut her off. The sound of a whistle pierced the night.

Reluctantly, the soldier let go of Amanda and, remembering why he was there, he set off after José. No longer concerned with the strange behaviour of three young tourists, Ramon and his troops were all now in hot pursuit of José, convinced the man they were seeking had broken cover at last.

A shot whistled past him as he ran, but José barely noticed it as he shouted at Nuala to stop before it was too late. Yet all the shouting and shooting only made her run faster. Suddenly the ground beneath her feet fell away and, for a sickening moment her feet trod air. Then she felt herself pitching forward and everything went black.

CHAPTER 10

Discovery at the Dig

José stumbled forward, Nuala's body caught firmly in his arms, as the troops closed in on him. So intent had he been on reaching the foot of the cliff before she fell that he was barely conscious of the pursuing soldiers. Only now, as they dragged Nuala's still unconscious body from him, seizing his arms and forcing them behind his back, did he fully realise what was happening. In Quechuan, Spanish and English he begged them to release him, protesting that he was no terrorist.

Opening her eyes, Nuala saw soldiers all around her and screamed for help. People were running from the hotel now and suddenly she was in the midst of a large crowd. Out of the confusion of sounds she heard Mr Houston's voice, loud and assertive:

'Let her go. She's done nothing. She's only a child!'

'Then why she run to meet this man?'

It was Captain Ramon. Nuala could see him now, beside a cluster of soldiers.

'I wasn't running to meet anyone!' she shouted. 'I was only running away from you, because you frightened me!'

'And I don't wonder!' It was her mother's voice now. 'All of you shouting and shooting like a pack of trigger-happy cowboys for no reason!'

'Was for very good reason,' Ramon declared. 'This man is dangerous subversive. Is for your own safety we capture him.'

Nuala struggled to her feet, shaking herself free from the now uncertain grip of the soldier who had been supporting her. So they had caught Juan after all their efforts. She looked pityingly at the man whose hands were tied behind his back. Then she saw it was José.

'He's no subversive!' she cried. 'He's one of the hotel waiters. He's hardly been outside the hotel door since we got here. He's on at breakfast, lunch and dinner, and if you ask for coffee or drinks in between he brings them. He can't have had time to do anything subversive!'

'Then why he run?' Ramon demanded. 'Only guilty man run when I order that he stop!'

'I run to save life!' José cried indignantly. 'Do you not see this girl runs towards cliff? I get there one second later she break her neck!'

'Is true!'

At the sound of his voice, everyone turned to see the hotel manager on the fringe of the crowd.

'José and I see her run from kitchen. I think what to do, but already José is running. He very brave man!'

113

'And deserves all our thanks!' It was Mr Houston again, as Nuala's mother ran to her and held her close.

'He deserves a medal!' she cried indignantly, 'instead of being manhandled by you lot who can't tell the difference between a subversive and a hero!'

For a moment Nuala was scared that Captain Ramon might arrest her mother, considering the picture Mr Houston had painted of the Peruvian army.

Mr Houston took Ramon aside and Nuala thought she heard the rustle of bank notes. Then Ramon ordered his man to let José go, Nuala's mother thanked José for what he'd done and they all went back to the hotel, where Mrs Houston was waiting.

'Is Amanda not with you?' she asked, before they could tell her what had happened.

'I thought she was with José,' Nuala said. 'She was somewhere by the back door when Kevin and I went out.'

'Which you'd no business doing,' her mother said severely. 'Hadn't you been warned to stay indoors? And where's Kevin now?'

'I don't really know,' Nuala admitted. 'He was with Juan.'

'What!' her mother screamed in horror. 'Is he out of his mind? We must find him at once!'

But at that moment Kevin strolled into the lounge. His clothes were untidy, with cactus prickles sticking to his shirt and hair, but otherwise he seemed much as usual.

'Oh, thank God!' his mother cried. 'Wherever were you?'

'I went as far as the Inca trail with Juan,' Kevin said casually. 'By then everyone seemed to have lost interest in us, so I figured he'd be okay on his own. I shook hands with him, wished him luck and came on home. He should be well on his way to Huinay Huayna by now.'

'Great! I'm so glad he got away,' Nuala cried. 'That's what I hoped would happen. I mean, I knew if I ran they'd all be looking at me!'

'Are you saying you were only pretending to be scared?' her mother asked.

Nuala nodded, smiling, but Kevin grinned rudely.

'That wasn't how it looked from where I was standing,' he told her.

Nuala began to protest, but her mother only shouted at her that she could have been killed and if she had only been pretending what she had done was even more stupid. Meanwhile, Mrs Houston had rounded on Kevin.

'Well, have *you* seen my daughter?' she demanded.

'Not since we were all together in the kitchen,' he said. 'D'you want me to go and look for her?'

'I'm gonna look for her myself,' she announced and marched out of the lounge with a look on her face that suggested Amanda might be in serious trouble. But, when she reached the kitchens, she didn't immediately recognise her daughter in the bedraggled figure hanging over the scullery sink in soiled white overalls.

'Pardon me,' she said, 'but do you speak English?'

Amanda turned at the sound of her mother's voice.

'I guess so, Momma,' she said, trying to smile, but her voice shook a little. Mrs Houston could hardly believe that this was her cool, sophisticated daughter.

'Lord's sakes!' she cried, 'Is that you, honey? And what on earth are you doing in those ghastly clothes?'

'I don't have anything else to wear, Momma,' Amanda confessed. 'I was waiting till there was no one around so's I could get up to my room without anyone seeing me. Are the soldiers gone?'

'I'm thankful to say they are,' her mother replied. 'But what ever happened to your pink top? Did you spill something down it?'

'I guess we'll never see that again, Momma,' Amanda said sadly, for she had liked the pink and lavender top. 'I reckon it could be half-way to Huinay Huayna by now.'

Her mother looked at her puzzled.

'How d'you figure that, honey?' she asked.

'I swapped clothes with Juan,' Amanda told her. 'So everyone would think he was me.'

'How could you do such a thing?' her mother cried, scandalised. 'That pretty pink suit you spent half the day downtown choosing!'

'I know, Momma,' Amanda said, 'but please don't shout at me. I don't feel well.'

She sounded close to tears and her mother decided she must be sickening for something.

'Here, honey!' she told her, taking the shawl from around her own shoulders. 'Put this on and go to your room. I'll bring you up some hot milk.'

'I don't want it, Momma,' she said. 'I'd only throw it up. I already threw up in the sink. I guess I'll just go to bed.'

'You look kinda white-faced,' her mother told her, worried. 'I hope you haven't picked up some bug. The dear knows what you might get in this god-forsaken dump and I guess there's no doctor this side of Cuzco.'

But by the next day Amanda seemed none the worse for her adventures, though perhaps a little less ready to show off her superior knowledge to Kevin and Nuala. And the whole episode was almost forgotten a week later when her father came back from the dig with news of a great discovery. Of course, they all had to go to Machu Marca to see it, and there Nuala found that it was all to do with the circular wall they had discovered the day they had worked on the dig themselves.

What they had thought was simply a circular-walled Inca temple, like the Temple of the Sun at Machu Picchu, had turned out to be the remains of an eight-storey building shaped like two letter 'U's, facing towards each other. Even Kevin was excited when they found decoration on the inside walls in vivid reds, blues and blacks, with a frieze made from the bodies of large red jag ars going all the way round the outer courtyard.

In the weeks that followed, they uncovered two stepped pyramids and a number of houses, grouped around a square which Mr Houston called 'the plaza'.

'These were built at least three thousand years before

Machu Picchu,' Kevin's mother told him excitedly. 'We have every reason now for calling it Machu Marca, "The Ancient City".'

'I like the jaguars best,' Nuala said. 'The ones all round the outside of the big building.'

'That's the temple,' her mother told her. 'The pre-Colombian race that worshipped there lived long before the Incas, or the Aztecs in Mexico – even before the Mayans. It's a wonderful discovery.'

'Will you and Mr Houston be famous now?' Kevin asked hopefully, but his mother only laughed.

'There'll be newspaper articles written about it,' she told him, 'and Mr Houston might write a book about it. His name will appear in the reference books and in the catalogues of the museums where things we've dug up here will be on display, but you needn't imagine all your friends will be talking about it. Archaeologists aren't like rock stars, you know. The only really famous one is Howard Carter, who found the tomb of Tutankhamen in the Valley of the Kings of Egypt.'

Kevin looked disappointed.

'It would have been deadly if I could have swapped your autograph for Jerry's photo of Sharon Stone,' he said.

'Don't mind him, Mum,' Nuala cried. 'He's only winding you up. I think the temple's much more exciting than anything in Machu Picchu. The tourists will all be coming to Machu Marca now!'

'I'd like the see some of those old wrinklies climbing

all the way up Huayna Picchu,' Kevin grinned.

'I expect they'll have to build a proper road up this side now,' his mother said thoughtfully. 'Wherever there's a tourist attraction you can be sure they'll find some way of getting the tourists to it.'

'That won't be good for the deer, will it?' Nuala pointed out. 'There'll be too many people and cars around.'

'Yes, I'm afraid it will be bad news for all the wild life,' her mother agreed. 'Still, luckily there are a few more remote valleys beyond this that they can move on to.'

'And it may force the government to find some alternative crop to replace the coca plantation,' Mr Houston said. 'They can hardly have people working it right beside the road, with archaeologists coming from all over the world to see it.'

'So long as they don't just arrest everyone working on it,' Kevin said, but Amanda shook her head.

'José thinks it may be good news for them,' she said. 'They'll have to build a new railway station twelve kilometres further up the line to serve Machu Marca and maybe build another hotel nearby. It's sure to mean loads more jobs.'

'And if they've a new station,' Nuala added, 'people who don't get work may be able to sell things to the tourists from stalls there, the way they do in Puente Ruinas. Maybe no-one will have to work on the plantation then.'

'That would be wonderful,' her mother said. 'It would be lovely to think our dig brought them something too, and that there'd be that much less cocaine on the market.'

'This calls for a real celebration,' Mr Houston cried. 'I'm gonna order a bottle of champagne for dinner tonight!'

Kevin made a face. 'What's the betting all *we* get is scraggy chicken?' he groaned.

'It's not chicken tonight,' Amanda told him. 'It's a sort of corn pancake stuffed with pork, almonds and raisins, wrapped in banana leaves. I saw it being prepared when I was talking to José.'

'Tamales!' cried Mr Houston. 'That's a real Peruvian speciality. You'll love them. The Hotel de Turistas is excelling itself. This will be a feast to remember.'

Other books from
THE O'BRIEN PRESS

AMELIA
Siobhán Parkinson

Almost thirteen, Amelia Pim, daughter of a wealthy Dublin
Quaker family, loves frocks and parties – but now she
must learn to live with poverty and the disgrace of a
mother arrested for suffragette activities.

Paperback £3.99

THE CHIEFTAIN'S DAUGHTER
Sam McBratney

A boy fostered with a remote Irish tribe 1500 years ago
becomes involved in a local feud and with the fate of his
beloved Frann, the Chieftain's daughter.

Paperback £3.99

MISSING SISTERS
Gregory Maguire

In a fire in a holiday home, Alice's favourite nun is injured
and disappears to hospital. Back at the orphanage, Alice
is faced with difficult choices, then a surprise enters her
life when she meets a girl called Miami.

Paperback £3.99

CHEROKEE
Creina Mansfield

Gene's grandfather Cherokee is a famous jazz musician
and Gene travels the world with him. He loves the life and
his only ambition is to be a musician too. But his aunt has
other plans!

Paperback £3.99

COULD THIS BE LOVE? I WONDERED
Marilyn Taylor

First love for Jackie is full of anxiety, hope, discovery. Kev *seems* to be interested in her, but is he really? Why is he withdrawn? And what can she do about Sinead?

Paperback £3.99

UNDER THE HAWTHORN TREE
Marita Conlon-McKenna

Eily, Michael and Peggy are left without parents when the Great Famine strikes. They set out on a long and dangerous journey to find the great-aunts their mother told them about in her stories.

Paperback £3.99

WILDFLOWER GIRL
Marita Conlon-McKenna

Peggy, from *Under the Hawthorn Tree*, is now thirteen and must leave Ireland for America. After a terrible journey on board ship, she arrives in Boston. What kind of life will she find there?

Hardback £6.95 Paperback £4.50

THE BLUE HORSE
Marita Conlon-McKenna

When their caravan burns down, Katie's family must move to live in a house on a new estate. But for Katie, this means trouble. Is she strong enough to deal with the new situation?

Paperback £3.99

NO GOODBYE
Marita Conlon-McKenna

When their mother leaves, the four children and their father must learn to cope without her. It is a trial separation between their parents. Gradually, they all come to deal with it in their own way.

Paperback £3.99

THE HUNTER'S MOON
Orla Melling

Cousins Findabhair and Gwen defy an ancient law at Tara, and Findabhair is abducted. In a sequence of amazing happenings, Gwen tries to retrieve her cousin from the Otherworld.

Paperback £3.99

THE SINGING STONE
Orla Melling

A gift of ancient books sparks off a visit to Ireland by a young girl. Her destiny becomes clear – *she* has been chosen to recover the four treasures of the Tuatha de Danann. All her ingenuity and courage are needed.

Paperback £3.99

THE DRUID'S TUNE
Orla Melling

In the adventure of their lives, two teenage visitors to Ireland are hurled into the ancient past and become involved in the wild and heroic life of Cuchulainn and in the fierce battle of the Táin.

Paperback £4.50

STRONGBOW
Morgan Llywelyn

The dramatic story of the Norman conquest of Ireland in the twelfth century, as told by Strongbow and by Aoife Mac Murrough, the Irish princess whom he married.

Paperback £4.95

BRIAN BORU
Morgan Llywelyn

The exciting, real-life story of High King Brian Boru and of tenth-century Ireland brought vividly to life.

Paperback £3.95

THE SECRET CITY
Carolyn Swift

When Nuala and Kevin visit the hidden city of Petra in the mysterious land of the Bedouin, they find themselves involved in intrigue and strange happenings.

Paperback £3.99

ON SILENT WINGS
Don Conroy

After his mother's death, a young barn owl is left alone to survive in a world he does not yet know. Who is the Emperor of Fericul who threatens him?

Paperback £4.99

CARTOON FUN
Don Conroy

An action-packed how-to-draw book which shows you how to draw your own cartoons – with spectacular results! People, faces, monsters . . . and more.

Paperback £4.99

WILDLIFE FUN

How to draw animals – realistically and in cartoon – and lots of interesting things about them. Full of fun and fascination.

Paperback £4.99

THE TÁIN
Liam MacUistin

The great classic Celtic tale, full of the excitement of the battle, and ending with the terrible fight to the death between best friends Cuchulainn and Ferdia.

Hardback £5.95 Paperback £3.95

CELTIC MAGIC TALES
Liam Mac Uistin

Four magical legends from Ireland's Celtic past vividly told – heroic quests, great deeds, fantasy and fun.

Paperback £3.99

HEROIC TALES FROM THE ULSTER CYCLE
Curriculum Development Unit

Classic stories from the ancient Irish legends – Cuchulainn and Queen Maeve's Tain.

Paperback £3.95

LOCKIE AND DADGE
Frank Murphy

Lockie is a bit of a misfit, and cannot settle in the foster homes arranged for him – until he meets a strange character, Dadge, who shows him a different way of life.

Paperback £3.99

OTHER WORLD SERIES

OCTOBER MOON
Michael Scott

Rachel Stone and her family move into Seasonstown House, and then the trouble begins. Who or what wants to get rid of them? A scary story, with a chilling ending.

Paperback £3.99

WOLF MOON
Michael Scott

Rachel Stone tries to get rid of a terrible curse – but can she and Madoc outwit the great evil they encounter?

Paperback £3.99

GEMINI GAME
Michael Scott

When Liz and BJ discover that the computer game they invented develops a deadly virus, they must travel into Virtual Reality. But there they find dangers they have never seen before. Can they make it back to real life again?

Paperback £3.99

HOUSE OF THE DEAD
Michael Scott

When Patrick and Claire go on a school trip to Newgrange, they release a power that threatens the existence of the human race. They must defeat it, but what chance have two teenagers against the ancient magic?

Paperback £3.99

MOONLIGHT
Michael Carroll

The body of a 10,000 year-old horse is discovered and a genetic engineer and a ruthless businessman dream of the fastest racehorse ever. Can Cathy outwit them and protect the new-born foal?

Paperback £3.99

THE LEPRECHAUN WHO WISHED HE WASN'T
Siobhán Parkinson

A tall tale about Laurence, who is tired of being small!

Paperback £3.99

THE DUBLIN ADVENTURE
Siobhán Parkinson

The excitement of a first visit to Dublin of two country children who see the capital in their own amusing way.

Paperback £3.99

THE COUNTRY ADVENTURE
Siobhán Parkinson

Dubliner Michelle on her first visit to the country. She may be cool, but she has a lot to learn about farm life!

Paperback £3.99

THE FISHFACE FEUD
Martin Waddell

A lively and funny story set in school with Ernie Flack, Fishface and their gangs. More about them in *Rubberneck's Revenge*, also by Martin Waddell, from the O'Brien Press.

Paperback £3.50

ALL SHINING IN THE SPRING
The Story of a Baby Who Died
Siobhán Parkinson

Matthew is looking forward to the new baby, but his parents have to tell him the sad news that the baby will not live.

A sensitive book which should help parents and children cope together with the pain of losing a baby.

Paperback, illustrated £3.99

And many more, for adults and children.
Send for our full-colour catalogue.

THE O'BRIEN PRESS
20 Victoria Road, Dublin 6, Ireland
Tel: (01) 4923333 Fax: (01) 4922777

ORDER FORM

These books are available from your local bookseller. In case of difficulty
order direct from THE O'BRIEN PRESS

Please send me the books as marked

I enclose cheque / postal order for £......... (+ 50p P&P per title)

OR please charge my credit card ☐ Access / Mastercard ☐ Visa

Card number ☐☐☐☐ ☐☐☐☐ ☐☐☐☐ ☐☐☐☐

EXPIRY DATE ☐ ☐ ☐ ☐

Name: ....Tel: ....

Address: ....

....

Please send orders to: THE O'BRIEN PRESS, 20 Victoria Road, Dublin 6.
Tel: (Dublin) 4923333 Fax: (Dublin) 4922777